Praise for

A Beautiful Evil

"If I could become a character in a fictional world, I would pick this one. Action and romance combine with good storytelling and an alluring world. More, please!"
—Melissa Marr,
bestselling author of the Wicked Lovely series

"Filled with action and suspense. [Readers will] continue to root for Ari's triumph over Athena, hoping that she breaks the curse that plagues her future." —*VOYA*

Praise for

Darkness Becomes Her

"Unforgettable, complex, and unique. I could not put this book down." —Christopher Pike,
#1 *New York Times* bestselling author

★ "An immediately and consistently compelling tale of a near-future New Orleans." —*Booklist*, starred review

"Part *Lightning Thief*, part *Twilight*, and part Maximum Ride." —*SLJ*

"A page-turning story with a multidimensional heroine and an atmospheric near-future setting." —*Publishers Weekly*

ALSO BY KELLY KEATON

Darkness Becomes Her
A Beautiful Evil

THE
WICKED
WITHIN

KELLY KEATON

SIMON PULSE
NEW YORK LONDON TORONTO SYDNEY NEW DELHI

SIMON PULSE
An imprint of Simon & Schuster Children's Publishing Division
1230 Avenue of the Americas, New York, NY 10020
First Simon Pulse paperback edition June 2014
Text copyright © 2013 by Kelly Keaton
Cover photograph of girl copyright © 2013 by Allan Jenkins/Trevillion Images
Cover photograph of gate copyright © 2012 by Thinkstock
For information about special discounts for bulk purchases, please contact Simon & Schuster Special Sales at 1-866-506-1949 or business@simonandschuster.com.
The Simon & Schuster Speakers Bureau can bring authors to your live event. For more information or to book an event contact the Simon & Schuster Speakers Bureau at 1-866-248-3049 or visit our website at www.simonspeakers.com.
Cover designed by Angela Goddard
The text of this book was set in Adobe Caslon.
Manufactured in the United States of America
2 4 6 8 10 9 7 5 3 1
The Library of Congress has cataloged the hardcover edition as follows:
Keaton, Kelly.
The wicked within / Kelly Keaton. — First Simon Pulse hardcover edition.
p. cm.
Sequel to: Beautiful evil.
Summary: In post-apocalyptic New Orleans, Ari continues her desperate quest to break the gorgon curse that has plagued the women in her family for centuries, but the relic both she and Athena seek to control is missing, amid rumors that an ancient power is on the rise.
[1. Good and evil—Fiction. 2. Supernatural—Fiction. 3. Athena (Greek deity)—Fiction. 4. New Orleans (La.)—Fiction.] I. Title.
PZ7.K22525Wic 2013
[Fic]—dc23
2013020649
ISBN 978-1-4424-9315-5 (hc)
ISBN 978-1-4424-9316-2 (pbk)
ISBN 978-1-4424-9317-9 (eBook)

To Miriam Kriss and Annette Pollert,
great champions of this book from beginning to end.
And to the readers for showing such amazing support throughout
the series. As the kids from New 2 would say, Merci beaucoup!

ONE

THE CRUNCH OF OUR SHOES ON ASPHALT, LEAVES, AND DEBRIS was loud in the quiet of Coliseum Street. Violet, Henri, and I had little less than two hours before nightfall, two hours before the February chill would invade the sun-warmed bricks and pavements, when blurry halos would appear around the few working streetlamps, when the predators, both natural and supernatural, would wake and begin to hunt.

We had to hurry.

A barely-there breeze moved through the Garden District. I saw it more than felt it; the jagged strips of Spanish moss waved gently from the limbs of old oaks. All the way down the street, the low-reaching limbs and pale moss created a tunnel of swaying, ghostly dancers.

The GD was a semi–ghost town, a ruinous, forgotten neighborhood populated by squatters, misfits, and other *things* that preferred to stay hidden. By day it was a beautiful, overgrown jungle, a strange mix of grandeur and decay—southern opulence turned rotting splendor. But at night the GD was downright still, as though the entire neighborhood was holding its breath, hoping like hell it'd make it to see another sunrise.

Lining the street were old mansions, some in ruins, some occupied, and some hollow and dark, watching and waiting, daring one to cross their eerie thresholds and lay claim.

To say I loved the GD was putting it mildly. As someone who'd felt lost and abandoned most of her life, this place spoke to me. In a weird way, I related to those old houses and their wild, overgrown gardens. They were dark and neglected—exactly how I'd been for so long. How I *still* felt at times, because, honestly, I had a hell of a lot of darkness left in me to deal with. Only now, I wasn't lost.

And I wasn't alone.

I'd found my home and I'd found my family.

When the city flooded fifteen years earlier, some of the water never receded from the lower half of the GD. In those areas, mansions rose out of black stagnant water. Statues, streetlamps, iron fences, and even the southern tip of Lafayette Cemetery had become fixtures of the shallow swamp. As we passed the cemetery, with its aboveground tombs and exposed bones, my stomach clenched. In one of those tombs I'd inhaled the ground-up toe bone of the infamous clairvoyant, Alice Cromley, and was shown the day Athena cursed my ancestor, the beautiful and devout Medusa, with an unjust, unwarranted punishment.

The cemetery had played host to our first battle with Athena and her grotesque minions. And it was the place the goddess had shown me and my friends a vision of the gorgon I'd one day become. It was a memory I wished time would erase, but so far, the memory hadn't even dimmed. The muted pain of what my future held had slithered beneath my scalp, splitting my skin as milky-white visions crept out, rising like weightless streamers around my face. The brush of their phantom skin, the hissing so close and intimate in my ears . . .

The memory had a knack for making my hands shake and my blood run cold. I let out a long, quiet exhale, shoving my hands into the front pocket of my hoodie and linking them together.

"I wonder what she's gonna do when he grows too big to carry," Henri said as we continued toward Audubon Park and the Fly.

I smiled at the picture Violet made as she walked in front of us. Pascal, her small white alligator, clung to her shoulder, his head facing us and bobbing with each step. His mouth hung open in that frozen alligator way, and his eyes seemed glued on me. Violet's Mardi Gras mask was pushed back onto her head. The white feathers on each side of the mask stuck backward like wings. She wore a black dress that came to her knees. Her socks were mismatched, one black with gray checks, the other solid black.

"Don't know," I answered with a shrug. "Leave him home with some raw fish and the remote control?" Because with Violet that could totally be a reality. She was a strange little girl with huge dark eyes, pale skin, and a short black bob that she cut herself.

And . . . she had fangs.

In the years since Athena had slammed her wrath into New Orleans with twin hurricanes, the Novem—nine of the city's oldest and most elite supernaturals—had bought the ruined city and its surrounding land from the US government. New 2 had become a sanctuary for all things paranormal, and an urban legend to those outside of its now privately owned borders.

But knowing all that, knowing my share of witches, demigods, and vampires, Violet was in a class by herself. A true mystery. No one knew what she was or why she had fangs. She never said. In fact, she didn't say much. But when she did, you paid attention.

That tiny kid with her love of all things Mardi Gras had stabbed Athena in the heart to save me. Violet had even lived through the horror of that same goddess trying to turn her into a gorgon, but the curse hadn't touched Violet, *couldn't* touch her, and when I'd asked why, her answer had been a simple, "It just didn't."

Eventually the swamp squeezed in on the debris-covered road. Brackish water spilled over in places, our shoes squishing on layers of soaked leaves and vegetation. A few cypress trees had grown up through the water, their knobby roots sticking out like rounded, black pyramids. Moss grew everywhere. It was beautiful to look at, but not something you wanted to touch, seeing as most of it was infested with chiggers and spider mites.

I could handle the swamp. I'd done it before. The key was not to let my imagination wander. That meant shutting down the fear and staying focused on our destination. Simple, right? Deep breath in, another one out. No problem. I slowed my pace and scanned the ground, making damn sure there was nothing coiled or hidden along our path.

"You know," Henri began, turning to wait for me to catch up, "I bet they're more scared of you than you are of them."

"Yeah. That doesn't help at all." I didn't bother explaining the nature of my phobia—true adrenaline-inducing, hyperventilating-causing, nausea-inspiring *fear* of snakes. It wasn't rational. It just . . . was.

A small smile played at the corners of his mouth. With his

flannel shirt, his long red hair tied back, and all that scruff on the lower half of his face, Henri was close to sporting a mountain-man look. "Figured I'd give it a try," he said, falling into step beside me. "You know you'll have to shake your fear at some point, *chère*, if you live out here with us."

"I don't live out *here*." I waved my arm at the swamp. "Says the guy who eats rats and snakes."

"I don't *eat* them, for chrissakes, just clear them out of buildings."

Henri was a shifter, an ability inherited from a distant, godly ancestor. Some people said demigods and shape shifters were one and the same, and the idea didn't seem far-fetched, not when you considered that in mythology many gods were able to transform into animals. Falcons, crows, stags, bulls, serpents, lions . . . Henri could shift into a beautiful red-tailed hawk. He earned money clearing vermin from buildings outside the French Quarter that the Novem wanted to reclaim.

He was good at what he did, being a predator and all. . . .

"Well, I hope they're paying you well," I muttered, "because that's just about the grossest job ever."

"Says the girl who's going to have a head full of snakes one day. The Novem could always pay me better, but it puts money in my pocket and food on the table, so don't knock it, seeing as how, you know, you *eat* said food."

I let out a sigh. "I'm working on the job thing. . . ." *Among other things.*

He bumped me with his shoulder, and I veered precariously close to the water. I bumped him back, shooting him a glare, only to be met with laughter. "*Pas de problème*," he said with a shrug, which I gathered to mean "no problem." "Not like you haven't been busy fighting gods and making a general nuisance of yourself."

"Ha, ha." But the reality went way beyond being a nuisance. My fight with Athena and my quest to end my curse had been a harrowing, brutal affair so far. And I didn't expect that to change.

"They wouldn't hurt you," Violet called in a dreamy voice. She'd turned around and was walking backward. "You're like their *queen*. I bet you could even control them if you tried."

"Yeah. No thanks." Not something I wanted to hear, picture, or even think about. Just the idea that I could control a bunch of slithering, rubbery, hissing . . . I didn't care if they loved me; I was *terrified*. Just seeing one sent my heart skipping and instant panic racing through my limbs.

I hated that I was afraid. I was armed with a 9mm handgun, a borrowed blade, and a power that could turn things to stone, and yet I was scared of a creature only a fraction of my size.

"Fear like that comes from somewhere," Henri said quietly.

I sidestepped a rotting log. "It comes from outrunning the hurricanes with my mother. You know what happens when it floods, when things are rushing so fast through the swamps and into the city? It pushes everything at you—fish, gators, snakes...." So many snakes.

"Heard about that. Covington and some other towns out by The Rim were overrun with them."

It was a memory, one of a very few, I had of my mother—four years old, running with her from New Orleans to a town that would eventually sit along The Rim, the boundary between New 2 and the rest of the United States. But as horrendous as that memory was, it paled in comparison to my mother giving me up to the state shortly after.

So began a long succession of foster homes, abuse, and trying to hide my differences. Though, for all my efforts, I couldn't hide my pale hair and eyes. Now I knew where I got them—Medusa. Her long white hair, thick and straight and shiny, and her eyes so bright they looked like the clearest Caribbean Sea, had attracted the attention of a god who raped her, and another god, Athena, who cursed Medusa for that crime. But in her haste to punish, Athena had made a crucial mistake. She forgot to exempt the gods from the gorgon's power. She'd created a god-killer.

Spying the dock and the boat, I let out a relieved breath.

Violet skipped down the stretch of rickety, low-lying boards and hopped into a metal boat tied to one of the dock's posts. She set Pascal on the only bench and then tinkered with the engine as I climbed aboard and sat down next to Pascal.

The boat dipped again with Henri's weight, rocking slightly from side to side. "Need help with that, Vi?"

"Nope." Violet eased past Henri and stepped onto an old wooden box. "I'm captain today."

She pulled her mask down over her face, as though she was preparing for war, not a trip down the bayou. The boat's engine roared, startling two snowy egrets nearby. Black smoke sputtered from the motor as Violet revved the engine a few times before reversing us away from the dock.

Henri smiled at me, lifting his brow. "Captain it is. *Allons-y!*" he called to her. *Let's go.*

We raced across the wide Mississippi, bouncing over the choppy waves, the fine spray dampening our skin. Violet guided the boat like she'd been born to it, and I supposed she had, being raised out in the bayous and swamps of New 2. She knew exactly how to navigate us to our destination—a secluded house deep in the bayou, owned by an old man, a trapper called the River Witch.

According to Violet, the River Witch was very powerful and knowledgeable. He was not in a coven, not a member of the three main witch families that populated the city, nor was he a warlock, which was what the few male witches in existence were called these days. I'd learned in one of my classes at Presby that there was a time long ago when all magical practitioners, whatever their gender, were called "witch."

The constant rise and dip of the boat made my stomach tight and uneasy. I gripped the metal hull with one hand, my other holding the edge of the bench, trying to stay anchored to my seat. Violet pushed the small boat to its limit, and I knew she was making up time. No one wanted to be stuck in the swamps at night.

We entered the wide channel the hurricanes had cut through Bayou Segnette State Park and Jean Lafitte Preserve. The bayou connected the Mississippi to Lake Cataouatche. Off the bayou were smaller channels, eerie dark places. Dangerous places. The perfect places for all manner of creatures to hide.

The boat slowed as Violet navigated down a smaller channel under a cathedral of moss-draped trees.

Strangely, it felt absent of temperature here. Neither hot nor cold. Just stagnant and damp, causing a film of humidity to cover my face. The smells of mud and decomposing sea life hung heavy in the air. A water moccasin slithered through the water, making serpentine waves, before curling itself around a small cypress root. Its body bobbed in the wake as we went by, and my skin crawled.

After a few more miles, Violet steered the boat into another narrow channel and slowed until we were coasting. Mist hovered over the dark water, and through it, a yellow glow appeared and a narrow boat took shape. It looked like it came from another time, another world. Made of reeds, the sides were low but the bow and stern curved high and inward to a point. A lantern hung from one of the curves, casting its dim glow over the boat. A hunched-over old man, his face partially hidden by the hood of a dark cloak, stood at one end, holding a long pole to push the boat forward.

I glanced down at Pascal stretched out by my side and muttered, "Looks like we're going to meet the reaper, doesn't it, boy?"

"He won't hurt you," Violet said softly over her shoulder. "As long as you don't touch his stuff."

Sebastian once told me that Violet had been raised by a trapper who lived in the swamps. "Is this the person who raised you, Violet?"

This time she shrugged. "He taught me some things."

As we drew close enough to exchange words with the River Witch, the reed boat turned and moved deeper into the bayou.

Eventually the River Witch's house appeared, rising from the water on short, stocky stilts. It was one story, with a porch that ran the length of the house and steps that led to the dock where we tied our boat. Wind chimes and sun catchers hung from the porch's top frame.

"When we go in, don't touch anything. He hates when you touch his stuff, okay?" Violet reminded us.

"Don't worry," Henri assured her. "We won't touch anything."

Single file we went, the witch leading the way, our weight creaking the boards under our feet. Warm yellow light filled each of the windows and spilled from the door as the witch opened it and went inside.

I followed, feeling a huge dose of skepticism mixed with a desperate kind of hope. So far, finding the means to unravel the two-thousand-year-old gorgon curse inside me had been like trying to find a tiny grain of salt in a desert full of sand. The only information I'd found had been in the Novem's library, where I uncovered two stories, one Sumerian, one Egyptian, of gods cursing a human. And nothing that helped me much, other than vague references to "untangling" the curse words.

I hesitated just inside the doorway, surprised to find the front room crammed with antiquities, the sort of things that would've been more at home in the Novem's library than out here in the swamp. Shields, swords, helms, statues, jewelry, chests . . . all stacked with no rhyme or reason.

Henri gave me a gentle nudge. "You moving or what?"

"Yeah," I said, distracted by what I saw and wondering just who the River Witch was and how he'd come by all those things. He wasn't a simple trapper, a simple witch. That much was obvious. Wariness crept up my spine and tingled the back of my neck as I moved through the room and entered the large kitchen.

Herbs hung from exposed rafters. Mortars and pestles of different sizes lay on the countertops along with rocks, eggs of varying sizes, and jars of preserved animals and reptiles.

Violet crawled onto a high stool at the wide island, and spread her hands over the smooth slab of white marble as a cat jumped onto the counter, arched its back, and hissed at her.

Violet hissed right back.

I smiled. *Thatta girl.*

"So," the River Witch started in a roughened voice. He removed his hood and took up position across from us. His was an old face with prominent bones under paper-thin skin, wrinkles, and age spots. He had a proud-looking nose, long and straight, and sharp green eyes that studied us for an uncomfortable moment.

"The gorgon and the shifter come to call. You are without the Mistborn, I see."

We'd waited as long as we could for Sebastian to take the trip into the bayou with us. But he never showed. If we'd waited any longer our daylight would have been compromised. And we only had the boat for today.

A low, scratchy chuckle came out of the River Witch. "A rocky start. A rocky road. And maybe a rocky end. You prepared for this, gorgon?" He didn't wait for an answer. "Of course you are. You're young. Foolish. Think you can do anything, you and your friends, you and your Mistborn *vampire*." He made a sarcastic flourish with his hands. "Romance . . . ," he sneered before grabbing a ladle from the counter behind him, muttering under his breath. "Nothing but trouble. Heartache that lasts millennia. Violet, bring me that jar of oil behind you."

Violet went to the shelf and lifted a fat glass jar, bumping an adjacent clay jar. A tiny, muted squeak erupted, followed by scratching and scrambling, like a bird trapped in a chimney. Two other jars next to it, both clay, both secured with lids, began the same kind of racket. The witch shouted an irritated command, and they stopped as Violet hefted the jar onto the table.

"Special gorgon," the witch said, taking off the lid. "God-killer. Powers before your time. Powers to do what others could not. That is important. So important." He dipped the ladle into the oil. "This . . . Hmm. This is the good stuff." He laughed as though his words were a joke. His head lifted. "How old are you?"

"Seventeen."

He returned to his task. "Not long then. Not long until you turn gorgon for good. That's why you're here. To find out if I can lift your curse."

"Or if you know someone who can," I said, trying to keep the skepticism from my voice.

His shoulders shook with more laughter. "Oh, no doubt about that. I know them all."

The curse would change me forever on my twenty-first birthday—the same age Medusa had been when Athena had cursed her. That left me three and a half years to figure out how to *not* end up like my ancestors, who'd chosen suicide rather than become a snake-headed horror, or who'd hidden themselves away from civilization and from the Sons of Perseus, hunters Athena had ordered to slay each successive gorgon.

Fate played out with each generation. Somehow the line continued, despite Athena. Despite the hunters. It was a cycle that never broke.

My father had been a hunter. And instead of killing my mother, he fell in love with her. So the cycle *was* breaking. It had begun with him, and it would end with me.

It had to.

The witch lifted a large ladleful of oil from the jar and dumped it onto the marble. It spread out slowly. "Give me your blade," he said quickly, shoving out his hand.

I hesitated.

"Hurry. Give it to me."

I withdrew the new blade Bran, my teacher, had given to me and handed it over, grip first. The witch snatched it and sliced his palm. Blood drizzled into the oil as I took my blade back, wiped it on my jeans, and returned it to the sheath at my thigh.

Violet propped her elbows on the counter, rested her chin in her hands, and watched the blood mix with the oil as though watching dough rise or cookies bake.

The witch's blood began to swirl in the oil. The hairs on my arms stood as small blood symbols began to take shape.

"This is a form of divining." Henri moved closer, fascinated. "You're going to read the blood in the oil. The same way others read bones or entrails."

"Correct. But this is not just any oil, shifter. This oil is from the olives of Athena's first tree. The one she created to win the city named in her honor. Athens."

"How did you—" I went to ask.

"Hush, gorgon. The *how* is not important." The River Witch hunched over the oil with concentration.

I disagreed. The how was very important. The witch. His words. His connection to Athena, the artifacts piled in the front room . . . How could he know about us, have raised Violet, *and* be in possession of oil from Athena's first olive tree? That in and of itself was astounding. Why did I suddenly feel like a tiny game piece on a huge game board? The witch was definitely a player, but whose side was he on, and what was his motive?

"She'll come." The witch studied the oil, as though assuring himself. Then he raised his head. "They'll both come."

Wait. Both?

"She already came and left with a blade buried in her chest," Henri said. "Athena is either dead or wishing she was."

"No, shifter. She is not dead. Nor is she finished with the gorgon or this city. You have seen but a fraction of what Athena is capable of. You all"—he gave us each a long, measured look—"will soon discover what it means to stare war in the face. You must sacrifice your fear on the altar of protection," he told Violet, giving her a nod she seemed to understand. "And, you," he said to me, "you must find the Hands of Zeus or you will lose your family, your friends, your city. Athena will heal and rise again. She will make her twin hurricanes of years past feel like a summer breeze. Find her greatest desire and you, we all, just might survive."

His words made my pulse pound. I drew in a deep breath to steady myself. "You know what the Hands are?"

"Athena's child, frozen in stone like the hands that hold it, yes." The sneer in his voice was unmistakable. "And no, I don't know who the father is."

"So I find the Hands. Then what? Turn them over to Athena so she spares us? She knows what I can do. She'll want me to resurrect her child." And then she'd kill me afterward. Letting a god-killer run loose was a risk she wouldn't tolerate. I leaned forward, gripping the edge of the marble countertop. "I need to find someone who can undo the words she cursed me with now."

The old witch's stare collided with mine in a contest of wills. His eyes glinted. I could almost see his mind calculating. Finally he shifted. "Of course you do. Of course. You find the Hands, return them here to me, and I will lift your curse myself."

I blinked, immediately suspicious. It was too easy. "No offense, but how do I know you can?"

He straightened, his chest puffing out as if I'd pricked his ego. "I trained with Hecate herself, a goddess older than the Olympians and far more powerful. Doubt me if you must, young gorgon. You bring the Hands to me or give them to Athena. The choice is yours."

I didn't like the River Witch, though I couldn't exactly pinpoint a specific reason. He'd raised Violet, which was a point in his favor, but he was also cunning and obviously kept his secrets and motives close to his heart.

"I don't know where to start," I finally said, but my guess was on Josephine Arnaud, Novem council member and head of the Arnaud family of vampires. She had either hidden them in the vast dimension of the Novem's library, placed them somewhere else, or destroyed them.

"You must look to the knowledge of the Novem. You must ask yourself why the Bloodborn Queen cares so much. What is she after? What does she hope to gain?"

Bloodborn Queen?

"Josephine is a queen?" Violet asked, intrigued.

The witch chuckled. "Josephine Arnaud." He stuck his pointer finger into the oil and swirled it around in a circle. "There was a time, long ago, when vampire kings and queens ruled their kind in Europe. Unknown to humans, of course. Long, long ago. The Arnaud family once ruled the vampires in France; they once held human titles and lands, immersing themselves in the affairs of the country. Josephine's grandfather was instrumental in seeing the rise of the Capetian dynasty over the Carolingians in the tenth century. Had times not changed, had god wars not come and gone, had vampires not retreated further and further away from human affairs and fought among themselves, she would be queen of the French vampires. But such is life. . . ."

I could see it. Josephine acted like a queen and would gladly rule over all of New 2 if she could.

"Titles mean nothing these days," the witch said wistfully.

Two weeks ago in the ruins, during our last battle, Athena had demanded the return of Anesidora's Jar, the name for the mythical Pandora's Box, along with the original contents that were inside it when the jar was gifted to the Novem. Those contents I now knew to be the Hands of Zeus. During the exchange between Athena and the Novem, it was clear that Josephine knew more about the "original contents" than anyone else. It wasn't a jump to conclude that Josephine had something to do with their disappearance.

And apparently, the River Witch thought so too.

"So Josephine is our target," Henri said. I glanced at him and he shrugged. "She's probably got the Hands or knows where they are. Obviously she has some sort of beef with Athena. Makes sense she'd take what Athena wants."

The River Witch stayed quiet, returning his attention to the blood symbols. If he was telling the truth, if he could untangle my curse, then getting the Hands was all that mattered.

Hope stirred in my chest, but I tamped it down. No reason to trust in him just yet. He knew too much and was somehow connected to what was going on. Until I knew how, I'd keep him at arm's length.

I watched as he dragged a finger through the bloody oil, then reached over the counter and drew a symbol on Violet's cheek with the same finger. "Your day is coming, little one. Just like we talked about; face fear head-on. Putting yourself in harm's way can be a glorious thing."

Violet didn't flinch or blink. She simply stared at the wrinkled old face, either understanding his words and accepting them, or not caring what he said. But I cared, and it frightened me to the core. I moved closer to her, not liking his ominous words one bit. I felt Henri stiffen beside me.

"Leave her alone," I said. "She's just a kid."

The witch's head canted slowly in my direction, and for a long moment, he said nothing. "Unlike you, Violet is not afraid. She will know her destiny when the time comes. Question is, will you?"

TWO

THIRST STABBED HIM IN THE GUT. IT WAS A TIGHT, TWISTING *pain, a cold burn that stole his breath and seared his insides. The soft glow of the streetlamps blended with the neon from storefront windows. Tourists and locals walked the car-less French Quarter street, their voices mingling with music and conversation from bars and restaurants.*

Those tourists, those few hundred who'd been granted entrance to the Quarter for Mardi Gras season, had no idea what walked among them. If they knew their blood called to him, sang to him, a lure so strong and tempting . . . they never would have set foot past The Rim.

The dark street scene in front of him blurred. He veered off the sidewalk and met with a heavy iron gate. The brick tunnel beyond the bars loomed black, but in the distance glowed an arched view of a dimly lit courtyard.

Dizziness made his view tilt. Just a small tilt, but enough to make him stumble as the hinges whined and the gate gave way. He fell inside, his knees and palms hitting hard against the brick pavers. The voodoo dolls and offerings tied to the gate's bars fell all around him.

Tiny bodies. All around.

He laughed.

Bodies were littered in his wake. That's what he was. Pure destruction.

He'd thought he was a freak before, being the child of a vampire and a warlock, but now the joke was on him. And the universe was a twisted bitch for sure.

Using the brick wall for support, he rose on shaky legs and stumbled into the courtyard. A sick, clammy sweat covered his skin. He knew he couldn't control himself, knew if anyone crossed his path now, he'd kill them, suck them so dry they'd wither where they stood. He wouldn't care who it was; it didn't matter. It'd taste so good.

Tears rimmed his eyes and wet his lashes.

His body gave out and he fell. With effort, he rolled onto his back. The massive gray house loomed over him. It was the only place he could go, the only place where those he cared about would never, ever see him like this.

His muscles finally relaxed and his eyelids slid closed. He'd made *it. They wouldn't see him. And more importantly, the monster inside him wouldn't see them. . . .*

The tap, tap, tap *of heels on the stone pavers woke him.*

The soft glow from the old lanterns on the courtyard walls burned his eyes, but then a shadow fell over him, and it didn't hurt anymore.

"Bastian." The sound of his name on his grandmother's French-accented lips was so goddamn pleasing it made him want to puke all over her five-hundred-dollar shoes. "I knew you'd come."

He tried to swallow but couldn't. "I need—"

"I know what you need, mon cher. *I know."*

Hands slipped beneath his armpits as two of his grandmother's servants hauled him upright and dragged him into Arnaud House, the great French Quarter mansion he hated with a passion. God, he was going to dry-heave. His gut tightened with readiness. He forced down the first retch, biting on his tongue, his teeth sharp and cutting.

Warmth flowed into his mouth.

Oh. God. *His heartbeat sped up.* So good . . .

But somewhere in his mind, he knew it was wrong. Knew he was going crazy. Cannibalizing himself. Yeah, he'd reached the edge and just fell over into Fucked-Up Land.

They stopped moving. His grandmother appeared in front of him, grabbing his chin tightly. "You fool." She glanced at the servants. "Hurry. Idiot has bitten his tongue."

Sebastian was dimly aware of barked orders, echoing footsteps, the smell of lemon furniture polish and the roses Josephine always kept in the house.

And then he was in a room, the mattress rising up to meet him as a plastic bag was pressed against his mouth.

The smell slammed him hard. Blood.

Blood.

Hell yes.

He sat up, grabbed it with both hands, and sank his fangs into the bag as his grandmother snorted in disgust. That first taste and he was lost in violent need. Lost in the taste, in the energy that slid down his throat. Nourishment. Beautiful, perfect . . . food.

He loved it. And despised it.

On and on he drank, one bag after another.

"No more, Bastian."

The fourth bag was pulled from his hands, empty like the three others before it. He fell back onto the bed, heart pounding, breath labored. His skin no longer felt clammy, but electric and hot, burning away the haze and filling him with clarity.

His teeth clenched. His eyes stayed closed, but he could feel his grandmother's gaze boring into him all the same. The last thing he wanted was to look at her. Josephine Arnaud. Head of the Arnaud family. Bloodborn vampire.

"We are Bloodborn," she began in a haughty, all-too-familiar tone. "The truest and strongest of the vampire kind. Your father,

your friends . . . they have no understanding, no experience in our ways, Bastian. I knew sooner or later you would come home where you belong. You are Arnaud now. This is always who you were meant to be."

He threw an arm over his face and laughed. She refused to see him for what he truly was. Not a child of two Bloodborn parents, but a halfling. Mistborn. His father, Michel, was a warlock, head of the Lamarliere family and, like Josephine, one of the nine ruling Novem elite. He hated the way she looked down at his father, even despised him, glad when Michel had disappeared ten years ago. What kind of sick person found happiness in a child losing a second parent so shortly after the first? But Josephine had been ecstatic. She'd thought he was all hers, to mold and groom. She conveniently disregarded the true nature of his birth and had called him one of her own.

He'd fought and rebelled against her for ten years, vowing never to become what she was.

And now look at him.

He'd never wanted to take blood, to lead this kind of life, to be an Arnaud. But he'd never been given a choice. Athena had seen to that. She'd forced his first taste of blood upon him, and after that, there was no turning back.

But he couldn't blame Athena for the choices he made now. Tonight he'd skipped out on Ari and the kids. He wondered how long they'd waited before leaving for the bayou without him.

Guilt turned his blood-high sour.

If his father, Ari, the kids saw him as he'd been only moments ago . . . He'd lose them. He'd rather die than show them this side of him, the out-of-control side, the side that didn't care. The predator. The killer.

"Bastian." Josephine wanted his attention while she lectured him.

He let out an annoyed sigh, removed his arm from his face, and glared at her. "Go to hell." Then he rolled over and gave her his back, knowing, despite how he felt about his grandmother and this place, he'd come back here to feed again and again.

THREE

DURING OUR RETURN JOURNEY THROUGH THE LABYRINTH OF the bayou, I eyed the ever-darkening sky with concern, tension keeping me ramrod straight. Twilight fell as the boat cleared the bayou and sped up the wide channel to the Mississippi, but I didn't breathe a sigh of relief until we were docked and on solid ground.

The four-mile hike back to our house was done in silence and absolute awareness of the darkness surrounding us. I took note of every sound, every smell, every strange feeling. And no matter what, we never stopped moving.

By the time we neared the house, my face was cold, my feet hurt, and my muscles were sore. Banging echoed through the neighborhood, the sound growing louder the closer we came to the Italianate mansion we called home.

Hammer on wood.

It had to be Crank, seeing as how she was the fixer of the bunch. She was the only one among us who wasn't supernatural in some way, and the only one who could fix an engine or a busted pipe, or rig the electricity to work. If not for her, there would *be* no working fridge, no flushable toilet or running shower. We still had to boil drinking water, and parts of the mansion were rotting away and off-limits, but Crank was indispensable.

I pushed open the squeaky gate, ducked under the vines, and headed to the front door. Inside, Crank was sitting on the grand, curved staircase, replacing a broken board in one of the stairs. Dub sat a few steps above her, watching and slapping a long baguette into his palm as if it were a mighty stick. He glanced up as we filed through the door. "Any luck?" he yelled over the hammering.

"Long story," I said tiredly.

Crank stopping hammering, lifted her head, and shoved her cabbie hat back from her forehead with her knuckles. Three nails dangled between her lips. Her head jerked in greeting. I returned her gesture with a smile, liking her capable, no-nonsense demeanor. Despite being twelve, Crank ran the mail for the Novem, taking correspondence in her old modified UPS truck across the Pontchartrain to Covington and picking up any incoming mail.

She was the first person I'd met from New 2. She'd picked

me up in Covington and gave me a place to stay while I looked for answers about my mother and my past.

"C'mon. Move," Dub begged her, nudging her in the back with the baguette. Her frown made him sigh loudly and run a hand over his short blond Afro. "I'm *telling* you this thing is hard enough. C'mon. Let me try."

Giving up, Crank rolled her eyes and handed Dub a nail, and we watched as he tried to drive it in with the baguette. The head of the nail stuck to the bread. He lifted it and shrugged. "A spike works too."

"Told you." Crank resumed her work as Dub slid down the banister. "We got food on the stove. Y'all hungry?"

Henri eyed the baguette. "Not if that's your idea of supper."

"Is it wrong of me to want to whack someone with this thing? I'm telling you, it'll do some damage."

Violet was already skipping into the kitchen, so I snatched the baguette from Dub's hand and followed. "I'm starving."

"Hey!" Dub leaped for it, but I held it high. I was still taller than him, but give him a few more years . . . Already his lanky preteen frame and wide shoulders hinted at the tall, substantial physique to come. With that suede-colored skin, those light eyes, and that blond hair—he was going to be striking. I laughed as he jumped and grabbed my arm, sending us crashing into the hall table.

"Mon Dieu," Henri muttered. "Children. Must I be the only mature one in this house?"

Dub and I paused at Henri's words, then looked at each other and laughed—"Yes"—and resumed our game of keep-away.

Finally I showed mercy and let Dub have his weapon.

"Uh-huh." He pointed the loaf at me. "You fear the smackdown. Don't deny it. I know you know who I am."

"You're insane." Shaking my head, I made for the kitchen and the large stainless-steel pot on the stove. The scent of oysters, tomatoes, and spices made my stomach growl. Steam rose from around the lid. As I got a spoon, the house suddenly became quiet. The entire time Dub and I had been goofing around, the hammering had continued. But now it stopped. No footsteps coming into the kitchen, no Crank. No noise at all.

I glanced over my shoulder. Henri stood by the table, a full bowl of stew in his hand, his attention on the archway. He, too, was listening. I met Dub's stare. The humor was gone. His hand tightened around his baguette. Violet, however, sat at the table, nonchalantly sipping stew from her spoon.

I crept into the dining room, which opened to the foyer as Henri went through the other doorway, which led into the hallway.

An eerie scratching sounded outside the dining room window. Thuds echoed on the porch.

The doorknob rattled. My breath caught. *Damn it.* I ran for the foyer as the front door burst open. Creatures with hairless, leathery gray skin, gnarled limbs, and rows of sharp teeth flooded inside. At least seven of them. Athena's minions. Her killers.

"Ari!" I swung around at the sound of Crank's shout. Her hammer swung end over end, right for my head. I ducked. It swooshed over me and slammed into the skull of the minion by the door.

Holy shit.

Breathless, I swallowed, giving her a stunned look as one of the creatures caught me from behind. Its teeth sank into my shoulder. I screamed, the pain instant, but so was the anger. I reached back and grabbed its leathery head, threw my weight forward, and yanked it over me, slammed it against the floor, pulled my blade from its sheath, and stabbed it in the chest.

Its piercing shriek sent pain flowing through my eardrums. I removed the blade and went for the next one.

Flames burst in my peripheral vision. Dub had set one of the creatures on fire.

"Damn it, Dub! Not in the house!" Henri yelled as he fought.

"I know! It was an accident!" Dub beat the burning minion back through the front door with his baguette.

I took a hard shoulder to the gut as one of the minions charged. The force pushed the air from my lungs and rammed me high into the drywall. The wall buckled with the impact. I held the creature's bony head away as its jaw snapped inches from my face. Over its shoulder, I saw Violet stroll out of the kitchen, wipe her mouth, and then survey the scene. Calmly, she pulled down her mask and crawled on top of the entry table.

Pulling my leg up, I managed to get my foot in between me and the creature and shoved it off. As it flew back, Violet leaped from the table onto its back.

The River Witch's words echoed in my mind. *Your day is coming, little one. Just like we talked about. Putting yourself in harm's way can be a glorious thing.* Damn it. I yelled at her to move, pushing off the wall to intervene when Violet withdrew a dagger and plunged it into one side of the creature's neck as she bit the other. It was savage and quick. And shocking.

I'd seen Violet do something similar before, and, like before, witnessing her violent nature firsthand was startling. Dazed, I glanced away and saw Sebastian striding into the house and toward me, blue energy forming over his hands so fast, the wind of it hit me as he gathered it to him. His gray eyes burned with intent, his face grim and his aura lethal.

I felt a minion at my back and ducked, just as Sebastian let fly his power. It hit the creature dead on, sending a shower of spent energy radiating overhead and leaving a glop of flesh behind.

As I spun back around, another minion came up behind

Violet as she released her now dead minion. I ran forward, jumped over the body she'd dropped, and landed in a puddle of black blood. I slipped right past her and between the oncoming minion's legs, grabbing an ankle as I went and flipping the creature off its feet. I scrambled up and stabbed it in the heart.

It was the last kill, and quiet descended again, broken only by the sound of our heavy breathing. We stared at the scene, taking stock. The attack had happened so fast. . . . I thought I'd have more time before Athena sent her goons after us. And honestly, I hoped, despite what the River Witch had said, that I'd dealt the goddess a death blow during our last battle. I'd stabbed Athena with my father's blade, which had channeled my gorgon power. My power had gone straight into Athena's chest and begun to turn her to stone.

The minions tonight were a sure sign I'd failed.

Apparently the witch was right.

Dub was the first to move. He sat down on the stairs. "Wow." His skin had gone a little pale. He rubbed his face as though he knew it, as though trying to stir his blood and bring himself back to normal—well, as normal as Dub could be.

I didn't need to look in the mirror to know I looked just as frazzled. I felt it in the shaky muscles, in the numbness and the chill in my skin. I straightened, pulling my blade from the dead creature at my feet.

Deep, even breaths. That's what Bran would say after one of our grueling training sessions at Presby. Slow and easy. My gaze stuck on Sebastian as he bent down and picked up Violet's mask, which had come off during the fight. He handed it to her and then faced me.

Nice of him to finally show up.

Ever since he'd become a full-fledged vamp, I'd expected Sebastian to go through some rough spots. Yet he hardly acknowledged he'd changed, even though the stress was written plainly on his face. It was in the haunted shadows lurking in his eyes, the tight set of his jaw, and the tension that radiated all around him. He was becoming more and more reclusive, withdrawing from me and the kids. Avoiding. I wished to God he'd lean on me, let me in, let me help in some way.

Footsteps echoed from the porch outside, drawing my thoughts away from Sebastian. As a group, we straightened, ready for the next onslaught.

Brown suede boots stepped over the corpse blocking the threshold. The boots went all the way up to the knees. Bare thighs. Leather skirt. Bow and arrows peeked over her shoulders. I blew a strand of hair from my eyes, relieved it wasn't another attack and yet wary as to what drama would unfold next.

Menai, daughter of Artemis, stood in the foyer. The tall, red-haired, sarcastic demigod—or god, depending on who her father was—surveyed the scene. She lifted an arched eyebrow as her earthy green gaze settled on me. Full lips quirked into a smile. "Still kicking ass and taking names, I see."

I wiped the bloody blade on the back of one of the minions and then slid it into its sheath. "The only name I care about is your aunt's."

Another figure, dressed in a tight black tank and black stretch pants paired with tall combat boots, stepped over the corpse. I recognized Melinoe immediately. It was hard not to; the daughter of Hades definitely left an impression. Melinoe's skin was two different colors. Her left side was coal black and her right side was a ghostly white. She parted her hair in the middle, and it followed the same colors as her body. She looked split in two. Black and white. Her eyes, though, were both an eerie, light bluish gray.

Violet walked right up to Melinoe and regarded her like an interesting specimen she'd found in the swamp. "You're two different colors."

Melinoe looked down slowly. Even the way she moved was eerie. "And you are but one."

Violet nodded thoughtfully and tested the name on her tongue. "Meh-lin-oh-way. You were at the temple."

"I was."

"You're Death's daughter."

"I am." Melinoe lifted her white arm. "With this hand I can rip your soul from your body and send it to the Underworld, leaving you but a shell, a ghost of your former self. With this hand"—she lifted the black one—"I can destroy that soul." Her fist closed. "Crush it until it's nothing but ash. No Underworld. No afterlife. Nothing."

Violet cocked her head and stared at her for a long moment. "Cool."

And then she skipped back into the kitchen, leaving us all a little dumbfounded. Typical Violet. Melinoe's lips twisted into a shadow of a smile as she watched Violet disappear.

"Were you shittin' her?" Dub asked. "Can you really do that?"

Melinoe's eyes went narrow and shrewd. She lifted her white hand and took a step toward him. "Want to find out, human?"

Dub ran.

Melinoe's smile broadened.

Menai elbowed her in the ribs. "Knock it off, Mel."

Death's daughter shrugged.

Menai stepped farther into the room and surveyed the damage. "Sorry about the mess. Our τέρας tend to get a little carried away."

"I'm sure you told them to be on their best behavior," Henri said with a frown.

"Where would the fun be in that? It's not like I *told* them to attack." Of course she hadn't. She'd said nothing, knowing they'd be true to their nature and hunt. Menai did Athena's bidding, but she didn't like it or chose it, and she probably figured seven less minions around the better.

My fists clenched with the desire to hit her smirking face. Playing with the lives of my friends wasn't something I appreciated. I was quickly learning that the gods, even the benevolent ones, had very little understanding of how short and precious and fragile human life really was. Easy to forget when you're immortal.

My ribs ached, and pain pulsed through the bite on my shoulder and along my back where I'd slammed against the wall. I went to the stairs and sat down, feeling pretty damn disappointed that I hadn't destroyed Athena.

Menai being here now meant she'd been sent. And I was pretty sure I knew what came next. "So what's she want?" I asked tiredly, flexing my sore wrist.

Menai's gaze lingered on Sebastian. "Last time I saw you, vampire, you were"—she grinned—"hard as a rock."

One of Sebastian's eyebrows arched with amusement. Whatever. I bet she'd been waiting *days* just to say that.

It was true, though; he had been stone. . . .

"Unfortunately, Auntie Athena is not dead," Menai went on. "She's in a world of hurt, which is nice for a change. But she has those who are loyal to her, and she is fighting your curse, Ari, and slowly winning."

I rubbed my neck. "And . . . ?"

"Recall your power from her body. Once the Hands are found, she wants you to resurrect her child. In return she will untangle the curse placed upon you."

I let out a laugh. And there it was. In the span of a few hours, two offers to lift my curse where before that notion had seemed like an impossibility.

"There is no one more able to set you free than the one who cursed you in the first place," Melinoe added.

I shared a glance with Sebastian. Anger swirled in his eyes. We both wanted Athena to pay for her crimes. She'd not only hurt us both, but she had also killed so many of her own monstrous creations, turning on them, using them, torturing them. . . . We had a better understanding of why she'd gone nuts and killed or imprisoned most of the Greek pantheon, including her own father and several brothers and sisters, and then going on to wage war on other pantheons. Her father had attempted to murder Athena's infant child. But none of that knowledge diminished what she had done. None of it.

It killed me that I'd stood right in front of that broken statue known as the Hands of Zeus. I'd looked upon those strong marble hands holding a basket with an infant child, and had never known the significance. Never known those hands were the *actual* hands of Zeus holding Athena's infant child, frozen in stone by one of my ancestors, and then broken off from the rest of Zeus's body and hidden inside Anesidora's Jar.

Athena wanted the Hands because she thought I could bring her child back to life. And she might be right. I had all the power of a gorgon, but I could also bring back to flesh that which had been turned to stone. I'd only done it once, and the result of that effort was standing by me with a frown on his handsome face.

"And once I'm fully human and she's healed, I'll be dead with the flick of her wrist. No thanks."

"She said you'd say that," Menai responded. "Athena is willing to offer blood-bound vows to leave you and anyone you name unharmed. I would suggest thinking long and hard about that, for your wording must be perfect. But she will make the vow, Ari. If you're the one to find the Hands, you'll have something she'd die for, has started wars for, killed her own father for. You will hold power over the Goddess of War. Think about that. As a gesture, she gave this to me to give to you." Menai handed me a glass vial filled with Athena's blood. "When you have the Hands, use her blood to open a gateway to her temple. Or send an emissary to set terms for a meeting. You might not want to visit our neck of the woods, given what happened last time. If the Hands are found without your help, she will send me to escort you to her temple for the resurrection."

I took the vial. "What do you know about the Hands?"

"I was born last century, so not much."

"And you, Melinoe?"

"I am much older. But I am forbidden to speak of it."

Sebastian crossed his arms over his chest. "Forbidden or don't want to?"

"I speak of it and I am no more," she said simply. "That was the vow I was forced to make to the goddess, like everyone who survived her war and ended up at her mercy."

"Are you forbidden to talk about who Athena was involved with before the war?" I asked. "Romantically, I mean."

Traditionally, Athena was a virgin goddess. But that was in ancient times, over two thousand years ago. And maybe back then she was, but so much of what happened between then and now was mostly unknown. One of a few things we did know was that she had given birth to a child.

"I should not speak of it," Melinoe said slowly, as though considering the repercussions.

Figured. I stared at the vial in my hand, feeling the warmth of the blood through the glass, even though it should have been cold by now.

"So?" Menai prompted. "What should I tell her?"

I was tired, tired of all the fighting and drama. I just wanted it to be over with. Maybe the best answer was to give Athena what she wanted, so all this would just go away. "Tell her I'll think about it. Tell her to leave us alone, and I'll look for the Hands."

"Good enough," Menai said. "See you around, god-killer."

Menai turned, coming face-to-face with Henri, who stood with his back and one boot braced against the wall. "How's the tummy, shifter?"

His hand went to his stomach, where Athena had shot him with his own shotgun, but his gaze stayed steady on Menai. Henri was definitely into her. "It hurts. You want to rub it?"

She laughed. Menai stepped up to him, cupped his jaw and kissed him right on the mouth, and then sauntered out of the house, leaving Henri shocked and infinitely pleased. "Hell, if I knew getting shot in the belly was all it took to get her attention, I'd have done it sooner."

Melinoe followed Menai, but as she went to step over the body by the door, she stopped and knelt by the creature. "Still clinging to life," she murmured with a soothing voice, like an angel of mercy.

The creature lifted its head, looking pathetic and hopeful. A pang of empathy went through me. I knew from experience that not all of Athena's creatures were mindless killers. Some were intelligent, starved for attention, or starved for an end to servitude and torture.

Mel ran her white hand over its head in a comforting gesture. The creature closed its eyes and shuddered, leaving me wondering if it had ever been touched so gently before. But it wouldn't see the angel of mercy tonight. Mel placed her black hand over its forehead. Its body trembled, then arched up as she lifted her hand, pulling a black haze with a bit of brightness in its center from the creature's head. When the haze withdrew completely, the creature's body went limp and its head fell to the side.

Mel turned her hand over, staring raptly at the soul in the palm of her hand. Then she crushed it in her fist. Light spilled from the seams in her fingers and then died out. She opened her hand, glanced over at our astounded faces, and blew the ashes at us like a kiss good-bye.

An eerie silence descended in the wake of her departure.

Dub sat down beside me and let out a loud exhale. "That chick's messed up. Makes the rest of us freaks look like the all-American family." He shivered. "Gave me the heebie-jeebies. She's even weirder than Vi." He gave Violet an affectionate smile, which she returned. At some point she'd come back into the foyer, and I wondered how much she'd seen.

"I like her," Violet remarked as she stared at the open door.

"Yeah, we could tell."

Crank stepped over the bodies, head down, searching. She stopped and pulled her hammer from one of the minions' skulls, made an "ick" face, and, muttering about how gross it was, took her hammer into the kitchen.

I got up, needing to shake off the creep factor Mel had left us with. "I don't know about you guys, but I'm hungry."

"Hungry," Henri repeated flatly. "Standing in a room full of dead monsters and you're *hungry*?"

"What? I worked up an appetite."

Sebastian's soft laugh drew my attention. "It's not like they're going anywhere, Henri. We can drag them into the backyard and burn them later."

We all went back into the kitchen as Dub regaled Sebastian with his awesome ironlike baguette.

Yep, just a normal day with the all-American family, I thought.

FOUR

THE IDEA OF DRAGGING CORPSES THROUGH THE HOUSE AND into the backyard was met with a lot of groans and muttered curses. No one felt like it. Especially after we'd just stuffed our bellies with oyster stew. But the bodies weren't going to move themselves, so we pitched in, taking a leathery ankle or a bony wrist, tugging the dead out of the house. Once that was done, we wiped up the blood in the foyer and the long, bloody smears we'd made dragging bodies down the hall.

I joined the others on the spacious brick patio. Vines grew high on the fence surrounding the property, some connecting with the low-lying branches of the banana trees, growing up over the limbs to make a green shield around the property.

Violet liked to go out there and hide under the leaves. She

reminded me of Pascal sometimes in her mannerisms, the way she loved all reptiles and the swamp, the way she scurried up things. . . .

I watched her as she climbed the back of a lichen-covered garden nymph. She put her elbows on the statue's mossy shoulders and laid her hands on its head, resting her chin on top.

The corpses should have left me disgusted and nauseated, but I was more tired and frustrated than anything else. It might be a small pile of bodies in front of me, but it sure felt like there was a mountain of obstacles in my way—my curse, the Hands, Athena, Josephine . . .

Dub snapped his fingers, and a flame sprang from his fingertips. As the flame grew, he blasted the pile.

Heat blew over me. I stepped back, shielding my eyes as Henri let out a whopping curse.

"Oops," Dub said with a wince as the brightness and initial heat blast faded, leaving behind bodies consumed in flames. "Sorry, guys. Sometimes it comes out of me too fast. Too much."

"It's getting harder to control," Crank observed.

Pink bloomed beneath Dub's cheeks. "Never used to be that way."

Henri snorted. "It's called puberty, dumbass. Everything grows. Powers. Hair. Body odor. Your johnson—"

"Jesus!" Dub yelled. "Shut up, Henri!"

Dub and Henri bickered all the time. They reminded me of

brothers—the banter, the joking, the one-upping and embarrass-ing each other. But this time Dub didn't give as good as he got. This time his irises seemed to glow like the fire that burned in front of us.

"Nice, Henri," Sebastian said with a resigned sigh, which made Henri roll his eyes.

"You might be able to fly, Henri, but Dub can turn your wings crispy in a heartbeat. So you better watch it," Crank warned, her lips set into a stubborn line.

"No shit," Henri shot back. "Which is why he needs to start taking his power seriously. Otherwise, he's gonna let loose and blow up the house or one of us. Yeah, I'm an ass. We all know this. I get on his case because he never listens." He stared at Dub. "Nothing I said was wrong. Your power is growing because you're getting older. It'll get out of hand if you don't learn to control it, master it now, before it gets too big for you."

Dub just stared at Henri, but the spark disappeared from his eyes and the tension seemed to ease out of him. Dub once told me there were people and kids on the fringes of Novem society who were special. Gifted. *Doué*, he called them in French. Not witch, or vampire, or demigod/shifter. Just . . . different. His abil-ity to summon fire out of thin air made him one of them.

Henri might suck at the delivery, but his message was spot-on. Dub needed to hone his talent or he'd end up screwed.

We all stared at the fire, lost in our own thoughts. Mine shifted to Athena's message and then to the Hands.

"You were right, you know," Sebastian said at length, his hands shoved deeply into the front pockets of his jeans. "About Athena. As soon as you give her what she wants, she'll try her best to take you out."

He lifted his gaze from the flames. His gray eyes were bleak. The concern for me was evident, but behind that was a vague despair. It was hard to look away; hard to stay where I was and not close the step between us and offer what comfort I could. He was struggling, and I wasn't sure how to help him.

"You should be the one making the terms, Ari," Henri said. "You're the one who can heal her. You're the one who can bring her kid back to life."

"Maybe. Maybe not," I replied. "I've only done it once. And Sebastian was stone for a blink of time compared to that baby."

"Yeah, but Athena thinks you can do it." Crank turned an old cooler over and sat on top of it. "And that's saying something, you know? Plus, she'll give you that vow. So if you word it right, like Menai said, then she won't be able to kill you. Or us," she added with a crooked smile.

"You can make any terms you want if you get your hands on those . . . Hands." Some of the lightness came back into Dub's sober expression as he sat down next to Crank.

"The Hands are your golden ticket, Ari," Crank went on. "You get those and everything will be okay."

"Yeah, no more snaky-snaky."

Crank hit Dub with her cabbie hat. "You're such an idiot."

"No, I'm *funny*. There's a difference."

"You hit one of those creatures with a loaf of *bread*," she pointed out.

"Well I couldn't exactly fry them inside the house. And it was a *hard* loaf of bread! Don't be insulting my Baguette of Terror."

The corners of her mouth twitched. For a beat no one said anything, and then we burst out laughing.

Dub grinned widely as if that had been his plan all along. He poked Crank in the ribs with his elbow. "See. Ain't it nice laughing by this nice fire?"

Crank rolled her eyes. Henri groaned. Sebastian shook his head, smiling. A campfire of corpses. Sure, real nice. But that was life in New 2. In the French Quarter you had the rich and wealthy Novem, the restored buildings and shops. Out in the wilds, in the swamps and the ruins of Midtown, you had creatures that made even the high-and-mighty Novem take note, and here in the GD, you had squatters and misfits and kids like us who did what was necessary to survive. If that meant grave robbing, stealing, whatever, so be it. There were no schools, no parents to teach right from wrong. What was learned was by trial and error, by life and death. I had more respect for the kids than I did for most adults I'd met in my life.

A breeze rustled through the high grass and weeds surrounding the large patio. Smoke blew in our direction. Sebastian muttered an oath and stepped toward the fire. Energy sparked in his hands as he waved them toward the flames, sending the smoke to the sky.

"Nice," I commented with a half smile.

He shrugged, glancing down at his hands. "Magic's good for some things, I guess."

It was good for a lot of things, things more important than shifting smoke, and Sebastian wasn't afraid to use whatever power he had to protect us and fight by my side. Much to his grandmother's dismay.

"Don't suppose you have any ideas where your grandmother would hide the Hands," I ventured, knowing the chances of that were slim.

"No."

Whatever I ended up doing after, whomever I bargained with, finding the Hands came first. That meant figuring out how to outsmart a three-hundred-year-old vampire queen. Joy.

Being the leader of the Arnaud family of vampires had obviously gone to Josephine's head a long time ago. She was full of herself; she'd never see reason. She had betrayed my mother and tried to destroy my confidence. She had it coming. No doubt, she had it coming. I'd had my share of setbacks and setdowns, and by my way of thinking, it was Josephine's turn. I was pretty sure she hadn't had a setdown in . . . well, ever.

"The last place I saw the Hands was in the library," I said. "So they must still be there, right? You can't take things beyond the counter. The Keeper won't let you."

"That rule might have been just for you. The rules for the council members might be different. Maybe my grandmother was able to walk right in, pick them up, and walk right out."

"So we'll have to figure out if they're gone from the library. If they are . . . it's going to be hell finding them."

"Yeah. She'd keep them close, though. She'd never venture into the GD or the ruins to hide the Hands. She has something extremely valuable and she knows it."

"In her house, you think? Too obvious?"

"Maybe. Wherever she's put them, they're guarded, warded, cloaked—you name it. And if I suddenly show up wanting some grammy time, she'll know why I'm there."

I laughed softly. "True. What about your father or one of the Lamarliere witches? Can they scry for it?"

"I'll ask my father. But I think the fewer people who know about the Hands the better."

I rubbed both hands down my face and sighed. I didn't want to deal with the Hands, but the alternative was worse. Josephine would use them to cause trouble, or she'd destroy them. If I didn't find them soon, Athena would send her own force into New 2 to find them, which would end up costing a lot of lives. I sat down on the brick pavers and crossed my legs, letting my shoulders slump.

"So we all start looking," Crank piped up. "I go to Arnaud House every week to deliver packages. I can snoop around, keep my eyes and ears open. . . ."

"And you've got an eye in the sky," Henri said, referring to himself.

"I got connections too," Dub spoke next. "When Spits gets a pricey selection of stolen goods, he takes them to the Cabildo or to some of the Novem houses to let the rich ladies pick from the good stuff. I can probably tag along." Spits was Dub's dealer. After Dub robbed graves, he sold his finds to Spits, who operated an antique shop in the French Quarter. Spits cleaned up the valuables and sold them to the Novem or unsuspecting tourists.

"I'll go back to the library and talk to the Keeper again," I said. "Last time I was there, he was inventorying the entire library in order to locate the Hands. Maybe he's found them by now or can tell us if they've gone."

And while I was there, I was going to start researching. I

wanted to know who had fathered Athena's child—and what part he was going to play once I found said child and possibly turned the baby over to its mother. That also meant finding out more about the prophecy that had started this whole mess in the first place, the one that said Athena's child was fated to kill Zeus. I'd need to talk to the River Witch again too. He'd mentioned "both" were coming. And I had to wonder if the other person he'd referred to was the father.

I looked at Violet, who had fallen asleep on the statue, her eyes closed behind her mask. The River Witch would definitely be answering some questions about Violet finding herself in "harm's way."

Henri, Dub, and Crank eventually wandered into the house, leaving Sebastian and me alone with the dying fire and the sounds of Violet's soft snores. He sat down beside me, and we watched until nothing remained of the minions but a pile of bone fragments and ashes.

Good compost for the yard.

The thought came out of nowhere. Once upon a time, I'd never believe I could hang around, watching a fire like this burn. It was macabre and bizarre, but that was my life now. Those bones and ashes were a stark reminder of how much my life had changed. It wasn't long ago that I was working for my foster parents and training to become a full-time bail bondsman like them. It wasn't long ago that I was as oblivious as the rest of the world to the truth about magical beings, about gods and monsters.

Sebastian leaned forward and wrapped his arms around his knees, linking his fingers together. A muscle in his jaw ticked. His Adam's apple slid up and down as he swallowed and then faced me, his misty gray eyes pulling me in like usual. A zing of awareness shot straight to my stomach. From the moment I'd met him, Sebastian reminded me of an old soul, a musician with an introspective, dark side. He was all that and more.

I'd thought him compelling before his change, before the blood, but now there was something more. His very presence could become mesmerizing if I let it. If *he* let it. It was part of his nature now. It made it easier for him to lure, to secure a person willing to sacrifice a little blood to quench his thirst. Even his appearance had subtly changed. His skin was paler, his lips were a bit darker. . . . His features were somehow more vivid now.

Tension filled the space between us, and I had the feeling he wanted to say something. Something that bothered him. My pulse kicked up a notch, along with the doubts. We were stuck at the very beginning of a relationship, unable to move forward thanks to everything that had happened with Athena. Since the battle in the ruins, Sebastian spent more and more time away from the house, and the time we did spend together, he seemed preoccupied and edgy.

Being the great person at relationships that I was, I had no clue how to handle things or what to say, if anything.

"You still having dinner with your father tomorrow?" he asked.

Totally *not* what was bothering him.

He bumped me with his shoulder, making me look up at him. "Nervous?"

"What?"

"Are you nervous? Seeing your father?"

Warmth stole into my cheeks. "Yeah. I guess so. It hasn't really been just the two of us since we talked in the garden at your dad's place." I drew in a steadying breath. "I keep wondering what we're going to talk about. And then I worry we'll just sit there in silence, which would be awkward as hell." All I really wanted was to get to know my father, to ask him a gazillion questions. Just like I wanted to do with Sebastian right now. How was he getting blood? Did he have a supplier, a partner who let him feed? Was it a she? Why was he spending more and more time away from us?

I rubbed my palms against my jeans. "How are things with your dad?"

"Fine."

The memory of sitting with Sebastian in the apartment behind Josephine's house, during her Mardi Gras party, filled my mind. He'd sat beside me and told me that blood was like a drug, an addiction; once you took it, it was never enough.

He'd never wanted it, never wanted to become a true vampire. Before, he'd had a choice. As long as he never ingested blood, his body would stay the way he was. But once he took it, he'd change. . . . He'd have to live on blood forever. Athena had known that; she'd tempted him to the point of killing him. And for what? To get to me.

"Sebastian?" I asked, unable to stop myself. "Are you okay?"

His silence raked through my nerves. Finally he glanced over and shrugged, pain clearly eating away at him. Why couldn't he say it? Why couldn't he let me in, let me help? "It's only been a couple of weeks since we got back from Athena's temple," I said. He groaned, not wanting to hear it. "You're allowed to be pissed off, Sebastian. You're allowed to *not* be okay, to give yourself time to—"

"Time to what, Ari? What's done is done. I can't go back, can't fix it."

He stood, paced, and then stopped, trying to compose himself. But that was my point. He didn't need to put on an act, to be *composed* and okay all the time. I wanted him to feel like he could be himself around me, to know that he didn't always have to be the strong, calm voice of reason.

"Sebastian . . ."

He drew in a deep breath. A tempest of emotion swirled in his eyes. "Just leave it alone for a while, okay?"

I opened my mouth, but nothing came out. We'd been through so much horror together, so much triumph, too. And now this thing . . . he was doing alone. He had every right, of course. I could understand that better than anyone. And yet, his reaction still stung. I'd tried to push him and the kids away when they found out what I was, and none of them had let me. They'd convinced me I wasn't alone.

I didn't know whether to leave him alone or to push.

"I don't get it," I said honestly. "You and I . . . we're . . ." I got to my feet and brushed the leaves from my rear. "A team. Together, I thought. I *want* to be there for you. I've never said that to a guy in my entire life." I stepped up to him, my throat growing thick with emotion. "I'm not hiding who I am from you."

His hands found my hips and pulled me close. "I don't want to hide either."

"Then don't."

He didn't say anything else. He might not *want* to hide, but he was doing it anyway. His head bent down, his cheek grazing mine. My breath went shallow. He smelled good, and it did funny things to my insides. He breathed me in too, deeply, and then his exhale bathed my neck in shivery warmth.

Seconds passed, each one growing more intense than the one before.

His kissed my forehead, my temple, my cheek, then paused, his mouth hovering a fraction above mine. I gripped his waist tighter. Our breaths mingled. I wanted him, this heat, this closeness, this connection. He didn't move, so I tilted my head and pressed my lips against his, the contact so warm and soft.

He moaned against my mouth, an impatient, desperate sound, before turning his head and delving inside. Our tongues met, hot and urgent. Instant desire flooded in, searing a path through my body.

And no sooner had it begun than it was over, leaving me gasping as he set me back and raked a shaking hand through his hair. He didn't trust himself, I could see it plainly on his face.

Heart thundering and feeling a little weak in the knees, I sat on the cooler, dazed by my reaction just as he was dazed by his.

No one knew how the child of a Bloodborn vampire mother and a warlock father would turn out, what powers they'd have, or when they would manifest. Sebastian's abilities manifested after I'd brought him back to life from stone. He had incredible power to control others, and the extent of that power had shocked not only those minions whom he killed—simply by telling them to stop breathing during the battle—but the entire Novem. I'd be lying to say it hadn't freaked me out a little when I first learned what he'd done.

Sebastian was worried, concerned his powers of persuasion could manifest through simple thought, through want and desire. Add that to the fact he was now a vampire, with a whole new set of wants and needs . . .

The fire collapsed. A skull tumbled out of the coals. Sebastian nudged it back in with his foot, then dragged a bucket over to me, flipped it, and sat down. He picked up a small rock at his feet and rolled it between his fingers. "If my grandmother hadn't hidden the Hands," he said, moving us back to our earlier conversation, "we'd have them by now, and your curse would be history."

"Too easy." I gave him a bland smile, trying to switch gears as well. "So we do things the hard way. We've done it before." *Not without paying a huge price.* "What I don't get is why Josephine has such a vendetta against Athena in the first place. Why is your grandmother so determined to hurt Athena, even if it brings all-out war to New 2?"

"Maybe there's something in my mother's things . . ."

Sebastian never really mentioned his mother. I'd lost my mother too, so I knew what that felt like, and I knew that sometimes, it hurt to revisit the past. "You don't have to—"

He tossed the rock into the ashes. "I have to look through them sometime, right?"

"How long has it been?"

"Almost eleven years. She died when I was seven. My father saved everything. And when he disappeared, it all just sat. Everything's still there. He hasn't touched anything since he's been back. I don't think he will."

Michel must have loved her very much. I hadn't been in New 2 long, but even I realized very quickly that falling in love outside of your own kind was frowned upon—especially within the Novem families and their leaders. Michel had lost his wife and then been imprisoned by Athena for almost ten years, losing his son during that time as well. Sebastian had grown up thinking his dad had abandoned him after his mother died.

"I'll look tomorrow or maybe after the meeting tomorrow night," he said.

"What meeting?"

"The Council of Nine. The heirs are invited. It'll be at Presby, since the council room is being redecorated. I promised my father I'd go." It was clear from his tone he had little interest in attending or being part of anything Novem. "He also wants us to do some training sessions together, learn to work off our strengths and weaknesses."

A crooked smile spread over my face. "He thinks we're going to get into more trouble, huh?"

"He *knows* so."

Violet shifted, yawning in her sleep. She looked so cute and strange curled around the top of the statue, her cheek resting atop its head.

"I'm worried about her," I said, and proceeded to tell him about our trip to the bayou and the River Witch's message. "He's tied to all this somehow. He's connected to Athena in some way. I'm not sure he can lift my curse, but he freaked me out about Violet."

"Sorry I missed going."

I shrugged it off, my thoughts still on Violet. "Back when we were in Athena's temple . . . You were blood drunk when Athena tried to turn Violet into a gorgon. But it didn't work. It was like Vi was immune or something."

"I remember. I knew what was going on, I just couldn't focus or do anything about it."

"She doesn't fear Athena, even though she should. Athena didn't seem to know what Violet is either."

"You should ask her." Sebastian and the others had already tried, but all she told them was that she was what she was.

"If she didn't tell you guys, I doubt she'll tell me."

"She might. She likes you. She's more animated, more outgoing when you're around. She talks more too."

I let out a tired sigh. "Maybe . . ."

Sebastian and I stayed until the coals beneath the ashes faded. Magic could be a very cool thing, I thought as I watched him use it to lift the ashes from the patio and move them high into the night sky. He swept his hand wide, and the ashes dispersed into the dark.

With a yawn, I led the way into the house and then settled in for the night, knowing tomorrow the hunt for the Hands would begin.

FIVE

"WELL, THAT WAS A TOTAL FAILURE. GOOD JOB, SELKIRK."

I shot Bran an exasperated glare. "Thanks." The table was not supposed to turn from wood to rock. A little mess-up on my part—too much power when I'd tried to turn a simple plastic cup to stone.

Cup and table were now fused together.

The only good thing about today's lesson was the realization that the training *was* working. It was getting easier and easier to call upon my power. And to control it. I stared at the table. Well, most of the time. Would that I'd had this extra training before—

My feet were swept out from under me. I was airborne for two seconds before I slammed onto the mat, the breath knocked from my lungs. "Jesus!"

A frowning face came into view. "You want to daydream, then don't waste my time, Selkirk. I have better things to do."

He didn't offer me a hand up, just stepped back, crossed his arms over his chest, and waited for me to get up. "I wasn't day-dreaming." One brown eyebrow arched. "Okay. Fine. I was. Sort of. But it was still about training," I muttered, getting up.

"Oh, this should be good. What about *training*?"

I really didn't want to share, but since he asked, telling him would be a hell of a lot easier than skirting around what was on my mind. "I was just wishing I'd had more time to train before I went to rescue Violet and my father from Athena's temple." I'd been unprepared, and so much had gone wrong. Henri getting shot, Sebastian being turned into a vampire . . .

An unsympathetic, slightly bored expression crossed Bran's tanned face. "So what were you supposed to do exactly? Not go? Say, 'Gee, sorry, guys, but I'm going to take a few weeks to hone my skills; hope you're not dead by the time I'm ready to rescue you'? Athena not torturing and threatening to kill your father and Violet until you were good and prepared to face her . . . that would've been convenient, wouldn't it?" He rolled his eyes. "Sometimes you can't wait. Can we get back to work now, or do you need more psychobabble from Dr. Bran?"

There were just some people in life you wanted to hit and hug, laugh with and scream at. Bran was one of those people. He got under my skin at every opportunity. He took great pleasure in egging me on, pissing me off, and knocking me down. And then he'd display pride when I got back up and kicked his ass.

He tossed a leather-bound book on the table. "Do this one."

With a sigh, I picked it up. "*Little Women?*"

An evil grin split his face.

I shook my head, biting back my own smile. Bran had wormed his way into my heart with his tough-as-nails attitude, insight, and sick sense of humor. He was a demigod, a leader and a warrior. He was the grandson of a Celtic war god, and one of the nine Novem heads that ruled the city. And he was my instructor of all things kick-ass.

Except today, when I was turning cups and little women to stone.

This should have been my last class of the day, but training had been pushed back until after school due to a conflict in Bran's schedule. It was nearly dark outside, and my stomach was grumbling. And turning things into rock for thirty minutes had worn on my nerves. I wanted to hit something, to sweat, to take the Big Guy down a peg or two—or at least enjoy the attempt.

"This is the last one," I warned him before closing my eyes.

I drew in a deep breath and pictured the book in my mind, focusing on my center and opening myself up to my power. I called it, drawing it, letting it grow and electrify my entire body.

It was a creepy, slithery sensation that took some getting used to.

Directing the energy down my arm and out my hand was a simple thing this time. The power snaking under my skin made me rub my arm and hand when I was done.

Bran didn't seem impressed. "You're a regular circus act, Selkirk. I should start taking you to parties."

"Yeah, we'd make a good pair. Stone girl and meathead," I said flatly. "We could even charge." I glanced at the clock as Bran snorted. "I'm meeting my father in fifteen."

Bran unfolded his arms and moved his head from side to side, stretching his neck. He cracked his knuckles and nodded toward the clock on the wall. "Think you can last for ten?"

With a wide smile, I shrugged out of my jacket and dropped it on the table. "All I need is five."

Sparring with Bran was less like training and more like being trapped in the ring with a maniacal giant. There was always a moment that began with my inner voice saying, "Oh shit, what did you get yourself into?" But then everything quieted and my reflexes took over. In the end, I wasn't sure who was more sadistic—him for doling it out or me for taking it and coming back for more.

In the girls' bathroom, I leaned over the sink and used a paper towel to wipe the trickle of blood from my left nostril, courtesy of Bran's elbow to the bridge of my nose. But I'd gotten the Big Guy in the solar plexus, and he'd had to hold up his hand to catch his breath.

I washed my hands and then unwrapped the thick bun at the nape of my neck. I finger-combed my long white hair, smoothed it back, and twisted it into a bun again, trying to make myself presentable and wondering why I cared. It wasn't like my father hadn't already seen me at my worst.

A faint bruise was forming beneath the inner corner of my eye. I leaned closer to the mirror with a sense of satisfaction, not minding the marks on my body or the aches in my muscles. They reminded me that I was strong. That I could hold my own, even against a Celtic demigod.

I did enjoy my training time at Presby.

I'd gotten admitted into Presby because I had something the Novem didn't have—the ability to fight their worst enemy. The school was my resource. It held a wealth of information about the gods: their powers, their early history, and some of what had happened to them in the two thousand or so years since the decline of ancient Greece. The rest of the world only knew myths of the gods from ancient times, *not* what had happened to them in the ensuing two millennia. That particular history might be lost to the rest of the world, but it was not lost here. Not with the Novem. Not within the walls of Presby, where kids learned every day about the gods, their cyclical personalities, and the War of the Pantheons in the tenth century that tore them apart and culled the god population considerably.

Most everything I needed to learn—warfare, tactics, magic, healing, control, information, things I needed in order to face Athena—could be found at Presby.

As I left the bathroom and made my way toward the steps, I caught sight of Sebastian. In his old jeans, faded black concert T-shirt, and aloof vibe, he stopped me in my tracks. The fact that he didn't *try* to look good, but managed to anyway, was definitely a plus in my book. And even though my instincts warned me that he was now a predator, I found it only added to the attraction.

He cleared the landing, a flash of surprise in his eyes. "Hey. What are you still doing here?" His face was flushed. A restlessness surrounded him.

"Bran had to move back my training." Sebastian had missed lunch, and I hadn't seen him in the hallways or in the one class we shared. I was pretty sure he'd never made it to school at all. Had he been at Michel's going through his mother's things?

"You doing okay?" I asked.

"Fine. Saw your father downstairs . . ."

I hiked the strap of my pack higher onto my shoulder, knowing he wasn't *fine*. "Yeah. Our dinner date. Never thought in a million years I'd say that." That I'd found my father after all this time; the idea still took some getting used to.

His gaze softened. "I felt that way about my dad too. Funny we both have them back after so long." After a pause, he leaned in and kissed me on the cheek. "See you later."

The kiss surprised me. The open display of affection, the quickness of it. He was already four steps up the stairs when I called, "Have fun." Sarcasm at its finest.

He paused, turning, his expression saying he'd rather have his toenails yanked off. And then he was gone, jogging up and into the shadows. He'd come and gone so quickly, I didn't have time to tell him that since Bran had moved back training, I'd had the opportunity to visit the library and speak with the Keeper. He'd found no sign of the Hands yet, but inventory was still in progress. For now, it was a waiting game.

Six

God, *he was such an ass.*

Guilt hounded him, sank into his body like a heavy weight as he jogged to the third floor. He could hear Ari's footsteps retreating. He'd lied to her. He stood there and lied *to her face, told her everything was fine. Fine. Was that word ever uttered in truth?*

It was possible for Ari's curse to be removed—needle in a haystack to make that happen, but it could happen. If only the same could be said for him. If only there was a way to go back . . .

But there wasn't a way. Vampirism wasn't a disease or a curse. It was a product of evolution, a divergence off the human family tree eons ago. Not every Bloodborn vampire drank blood. Not every half human, half vampire drank blood. Blood was simply the catalyst that changed the body. Humans who'd been turned into vampires were different; they had to have blood from the time of their turning and onward. But those born to vampire parents had a choice. If they could avoid the catalyst—ingesting blood—they'd never change. But it was so hard to resist. Most rarely did.

But he had. He'd resisted. There'd been no doubt in his mind that he'd never take blood. And then Athena came along. With the aid of Zaria, her vampire servant, they'd drained him, denied him food, tempted him with blood. Tempted him with Ari. And he hadn't been able to resist her once she slit her skin and offered to save him.

The only thing left to do now was try like hell to get a handle on it. For newbies like him, his near-constant desire for blood was normal. It'd take years to master control, years for his body to calm the hell down. He knew that. He knew all this . . . chaos . . . was normal. He just didn't want it. And he sure as hell didn't want Ari, or his father, or the kids to start looking at him differently. More than anything, he didn't want to see fear or disgust in their eyes.

He was torn between hiding his blood lust and saying fuck it, letting them all see. But he couldn't risk losing them. He knew intimately what it was like to lose, to suffer that kind of loss. First his mother, then his father, for a decade. After the day he'd had, going through his mother's things, it only made his decision clearer. He didn't want to chance it, not again. Not with everyone he cared about.

At the third-floor landing he paused, staring at the large doors that led into the assembly room. All nine members of the Novem council were inside. They were the heads of the prominent families who had long histories in New 2. Three from the vampire families of Arnaud, Mandeville, and Baptiste; three from the witch families of Hawthorne, Cromley, and Lamarliere; and three from the demigod/shifter families of Ramsey, Deschanel, and Sinclair.

The heirs would be inside as well. The next-in-lines. Some were too young to realize what a massive responsibility it was to be head of a family, like Bran's daughter Kieran. And some were far older than Sebastian, with families of their own, such as Nikolai Deschanel's grown son, Hunter. But others, like Gabriel Baptiste and his three cronies, were bloated on their own importance. If that was what the Novem had to look forward to, the council would not last long once the heirs took control.

Sebastian drew in a deep breath, placed his hand on the door, and entered. All eyes shifted in his direction. The Novem heads sat around a large oval table, while the heirs sat on chairs along the walls.

He met his father's intelligent gray eyes and dipped his head. He could feel Josephine's dark stare, feel her satisfaction, and he knew if he looked at her now, he'd see the small smile playing on her lips, the smile that said, "I've won. You're mine."

Whatever.

He went to the empty seat, wanting to get this over with as quickly as possible, when a chair grated across the hardwood floor and *a figure stood. Sebastian froze. Shock crashed through him, lighting every nerve. His heart started to pound. The figure turned and looked right at him.*

Zaria.

Memories flashed through his head, unbidden and unstoppable. Zaria offering him her wrist, tempting him every night in Athena's temple until he broke, until he became a monster. Her eyes traveled up and down his body, and then her lush red lips drew into a knowing smile.

Rage incinerated everything but his desire for revenge.

He was at her throat before he knew what had happened.

The council surged to their feet as his fingers closed around Zaria's throat. She didn't fight back. Her gaze remained glued to his, amused, calculating, challenging. He was going to rip her fucking head off.

"Bastian," his father's calm voice reached through the dazed fury. It was a sad tone, a tone that said he understood his son's pain. Michel knew what had happened to Sebastian, and he knew what it was like to be Athena's prisoner. He understood completely.

Another hand clasped his shoulder, and he shrugged it off violently. Someone grabbed his arm in a steely grip. It was Bran. He could smell him. His senses were on overdrive. All around him, he knew where everyone stood, who was holding back and who wanted to pull him from the bitch in his grasp.

He was panting. Red clouded his vision.

"You going to do it or not, Bastian, my love?" Zaria crooned.

The sound of her voice sickened him. He fought for control, fought to rise up from the rage and find his voice. "What do you want?" he ground out, his fingers easing on her throat.

"I didn't come here for you. I can see how upset that makes you, darling. I'm here on business. Athena's business."

His grip went tighter at the goddess's name.

"Sebastian. Let her go, son. This is not the time." Then his father's voice dropped to a chilling tone directed at Zaria. "There will come a time, that I promise you." His voice went gentle again. "Your revenge must wait, Bastian. Another time, another place."

Michel's words finally sank in. Another time. Another place. But soon. Soon, she'd pay for her hand in torturing him, in wrecking everything. He shoved Zaria back with enough force that she struck the table and went sprawling over its surface. Anger filled her cheeks. Yeah. She didn't like that, looking weak. She straightened, righting her blouse and skirt.

Bran and Michel blocked his path, but he angled through them without a word and slumped into his seat. So many eyes were on him, but he didn't care. His heart still raced and adrenaline still flooded his system. His knee bounced relentlessly.

After everyone found their seats again, the meeting proceeded.

"Well," Rowen Hawthorne said as she tucked a strand of long blond hair behind her ear, "that was fun. Now that we're all here . . ." Her attention went to Zaria. "Our surprise visitor has come via synagraphus, or safe-conduct," she said for the benefit of the younger heirs unfamiliar with the Latin term. "I hand it over to you."

Zaria drew in a breath and seemed to go right back into temptress mode. "Athena is not dead. Sorry to disappoint you," she said slyly. "She sends me with a message. As you are all well aware, she wants what was in Anesidora's Jar when it was gifted to your ancestors."

Sebastian sat straighter. Shit. He knew where this was headed.

"Athena wants the Hands of Zeus. Let's not play coy and kid ourselves. By now most of you have likely guessed what they are and why she wants them. But none of that matters. What matters is that you return what is hers."

"Why would we do that?" Josephine asked in a casual tone that Sebastian knew was far from the truth.

"Why not? You have no need of them."

Josephine drummed her perfectly manicured nails on the table. "I think we do. I think keeping the Hands in our possession keeps Athena in line. And keeps us safe."

Murmurs of agreement went around the room.

Zaria seemed unaffected. "And that is why Athena has offered Donum Essentia Dea to the one who returns her property."

Gasps echoed through the room. More than a few Novem went pale. Michel sat back in his chair, stunned. Bran let out a low whistle. And the tension in the room just shot sky-high. Sebastian had no idea what Donum Essentia Dea was, and from their confused looks, neither did any of the other heirs. Finally Hunter spoke up. "For those of us Latin-challenged attendees, mind telling us what that is exactly?"

Sebastian found it odd that the person most affected by Zaria's words was Josephine. She looked as though she was about to be sick, while Zaria looked like the Cheshire cat. Whatever offering she made had just turned the tables in a major way.

Looks of warning passed around the table. It was clear the Novem didn't want the heirs to know.

"All they have to do is look it up and put the pieces together," Nell Cromley said. When no one took the initiative, she pushed back from the table and stood. "Donum Essentia Dea is the act of gifting the essence of a god, or in this case, goddess. It means Athena has just offered everything that makes her who she is. Her immortality and all her accumulated power in exchange for the Hands of Zeus. She's offering to make one of us a god."

"She can do that?" Kieran asked her father in disbelief.

Bran answered, his deep voice resigned. "Aye. She can. She can give it all up and become mortal."

The heirs went silent. And Sebastian was no exception. Athena was willing to give up her immortality, to be human, to get her kid back.

Zaria gazed over the assembly with a satisfied expression. "I'd suggest watching your backs from now on." She pivoted and sauntered to the door, waving a hand as she went. "Good luck. You're gonna need it." And then she disappeared into thin air.

As soon as she left, Bran glared at each Novem head. "Stop. Stop it right now. Do not let this divide us. That's exactly what she wants, and you know it."

"The Hands are currently in the library, correct?" Simon Baptiste asked quietly, flipping a pen through his fingers.

A shiver went down Sebastian's spine.

Simon was known for his excesses and cruelties. He stayed just barely within Novem law, but everyone knew there were heinous crimes done in secret, things the group could never pin on him. His son, Gabriel, was fast becoming like his father.

No one answered Simon. They all believed the Hands were there. Sebastian half expected all of them to run for the door. The kind of power Athena was offering was staggering. Yet no one moved. No one wanted to be the first to show where their loyalties lay.

"We must agree the Hands stay in the library," Michel said, glancing around the room. "We must vow never to let what was said here go farther than this room. To do so would mean chaos, betrayal, murder, war."

"Michel is right," Rowen said. "This is our home. If word gets out, the library will be under siege. We'll be hunted for knowing how to get inside. Your heirs will be hunted for any knowledge they might possess about the library. We must agree to do nothing."

"What about Ari?" Gabriel asked. "She knows how to get inside. She'd be the one Athena or anyone else goes after."

"She doesn't know how to get inside on her own," Sebastian said, giving Gabriel a look that promised retribution.

"Sebastian is right. I let her into the library," Michel said. "She does not have the blood or the ward combinations to get inside herself. Only we do. But we must agree. We must not speak of what happened here tonight or we are all targets."

"Targets, or betrayers ourselves," Nikolai Deschanel spoke up. "Do I put my trust in all of you? Do I do nothing while the rest of you grasp at immortality, at godhood? Or do I strike first?"

The question hung suspended in the room. The Novem's collective energy became thick, making the room hot and stuffy. Sweat beaded on Sebastian's skin.

Traitor he might be, but Sebastian knew he had to get those Hands out of the library before someone else did—if they were even there. He wouldn't do it for immortality. He'd do it for Ari.

"We should give them back," Nell Cromley said. "Doesn't that solve everything? Just send them back before this whole situation blows up."

"The heirs can be dismissed now," Soren Mandeville said.

After vowing their silence, the heirs were let go. Sebastian was the first to exit, drawing in a deep breath of untainted air. He didn't stop until he was on the second floor. He was shaking, adrenaline still speeding through his system like a rocket. His boots thudded across the long gallery that fronted Jackson Square below. At one *of the arched windows, he stopped and dragged his fingers through his hair.*

Hunter followed and parked himself on the other side of the window, his gaze somber as he stared. Hunter was older. He'd been imprisoned by Athena and set free with Michel when Ari had escaped her cell, rescuing the lot of them. "Athena knows exactly what she's doing, I'll say that for her."

"Master of strategic warfare and all," Sebastian said dryly.

"She has it all planned out, every possible outcome, every variable. We're infants compared to her, to what she knows, her experience. . . . In other words, we're fucked, my friend. Dangling a jewel like that in front of the council . . ."

The low murmur of the other heirs filing down the steps made Sebastian turn toward the landing. "They won't all keep silent."

"Probably not. The Hands should go back."

"Not everyone is going to feel that way. My grandmother for one."

"Baptiste for another. Katherine Sinclair, too, from what I know about her. Mandeville, maybe . . ." Hunter looked at him. "What about you?"

Sebastian laughed at the idea that he'd want that kind of power. Hell, he didn't even want the power he had now.

Hunter smiled. "Yeah, me too." He went quiet for a moment. "This is going to get out. Having the heirs at the meeting tonight . . . goddamn bad luck. Look out for your girl. Not everyone is going to believe that she can't get inside the library on her own. She'll be a target for those wanting to find the Hands."

Hunter was sincere, Sebastian knew that. He also knew that in order to remove the target on Ari's back, he needed to find the Hands before anyone else. And that meant figuring out whether they were still in the library.

"The council will make a decision about protecting the library tonight. If you're going to get in, you need to do it now."

Was he that obvious? Or was Hunter just extremely insightful? He'd have to raid the library tonight while they were still up there debating. It had to be now.

Hunter slapped him on the shoulder. "Take care, Lamarliere."

Sebastian nodded and watched the shifter jog down the stairs before returning to the window.

He had a power very few beings had. He could trace, disappear from one location and appear at another. But he'd never tried going through walls or into warded rooms. He was only learning to master the ability.

Now or never.

SEVEN

My pulse thumped with anxiety as I hurried down the stairs and across the old, polished hardwoods. My father waited just inside the arched double door of Presby. Soft light filtered through the glass panes, highlighting him. When I imagined an ancient Greek warrior, it was my father's image that came to mind. He was handsome. Golden. Strong. Lethal. An old warrior in the body of a thirtysomething man who didn't look old on the outside, but old in the eyes.

We were taking it slow. No pressure. No rush to form an instant bond.

I liked that about him. He was patient. Guess he had to be after a couple hundred years in Athena's service. My father had done some terrible things in the goddess's name, things I never wanted to know about. He'd also been through hell and paid his dues. And he had the horrendous scars to prove it.

My palms were clammy. I rubbed them together as I caught his gaze. His expression remained neutral, but the slight, assessing survey, the quick study . . . The hunter in him couldn't help but take note. Designed to sense his prey, he could tell every tiny thing going on with me. Of course, I wasn't prey, but I *was* in his sights, and there was no doubt, even though he broke into a smile, that he'd detected my nervousness with ease.

Consoling myself with the idea that he was just as nervous as me, I stopped in front of him. My father had a good five inches on me. I wondered if I got my height solely from him or if my mother had been tall too. "Hey."

"Ari." His sharp blue gaze zeroed in on my bruise. A blond eyebrow rose. "I hope you gave the Celt a few of his own."

"Bran will be nursing a couple aches and pains tonight."

His lips quirked as he gestured for the door. "Shall we?"

We left Presby, keeping the conversation casual—the weather, school, training—as we headed through the square. The tall streetlamps had come on as dusk turned to night. Jazz musicians played. A group of tourists posed for pictures in front of the cathedral. It was a typical evening in the square.

We crossed Decatur and went up the steps overlooking the river. It was cooler there, the breeze brisker off the water, bringing with it the smells of river mud and sea life. My father paused at the railing and stared out over the choppy, dark water. Lights from boats and Algiers Point bobbed and blinked in the distance. "Your mother loved the river."

I went still beside him. *She loved the river.* The significance of having someone else in my life who knew her, *loved* her, hit me with a force that stole my breath. He'd spent time with her, time that he remembered, whereas my four-year-old little girl memories were few and far between. I had so many questions about her, about them; I wasn't sure where to begin.

My father glanced at me and smiled in understanding, then turned back to the river. "Our time was brief compared to the life I have lived, but those days with her, with you—they outshine all the others. They are always in the forefront of my mind, the things I remember the most." A long silence followed. And I didn't press him. He loved her too. That much was clear. He'd betrayed his goddess to love my mother.

As though he couldn't bear to look upon the river another second, he motioned for us to start walking. I fell into step beside him. "You look like her," he said. "You have her smile. And her frown." My throat went tight. Grief and regret and anger all jumbled into an angry knot in my chest. "She loved you, Ari. The first time she held you, she stared at you, amazed, and said, 'We did this. We made this perfect being.'"

I blinked. "You were there, when I was born?" His name wasn't on my birth certificate, and now that I knew who he was, it was understandable. But the fact that he'd been there with her, with me, came as a shock.

"Aye, I was there." He held out his hands, remembering. "I was the first to hold you. You were born at Charity Hospital. Eleni wanted to settle here, but we were always on the move, always one step ahead of Athena. Your mother thought the Novem and Josephine Arnaud could offer us protection, a home. . . ."

Athena had rained destruction on the city looking for my mother and father, the only Son of Perseus ever to betray the goddess. She'd wanted to make an example out of him. And instead of giving my father a safe haven, Josephine Arnaud had turned him over to Athena to stop the destruction.

"I sent your mother away," he told me. "When I knew we'd been betrayed."

"Have you seen her—Josephine, I mean?" The Quarter was small. My father was now sharing a neighborhood with the very being who had taken him away from his family.

"No. I haven't had the pleasure," he answered in a low, chilling tone.

Patient. My father was patient. And Josephine would one day be in a world of hurt—of that I had no doubt.

He held the door open to Maspero's, and we were seated

at a table by the window. Our waitress took our drink order and left. "After I was taken," my father said, trailing off, unable to finish his sentence. He tried again, and I knew this must be hard for him; he didn't strike me as a man who talked about his pain. But he seemed to want to clear the air between us. "I struggle . . . knowing what happened to her. What happened to you."

"She gave me up. She let me go," I blurted out. There. I said it. And it still hurt, whether I said it out loud or in my head.

"She was young, Ari, and scared of being found, scared of what she'd become. Giving you up was the only way she knew to protect you. From Athena. And from herself." He tried to smile, but it was twisted with grief.

I reached across the table and slipped my hand into his and squeezed. I wasn't good at comforting others either, but his despair . . . I felt it too.

"She'd be happy," I told him, holding back tears, "to know we're together now."

A small laugh escaped him, and he shook his head as though the idea was still unbelievable. "She would at that."

Our drinks arrived and we placed our order, though I had to wonder if my father had an appetite after all this; I knew mine was lagging. After the waitress was gone, I asked him if it bothered him that I was going out with Josephine's grandson.

"It's your life, Ari. Your decisions. I have not been a father to you."

"You haven't been a father to me because you couldn't. Not because you didn't want to. You do have input here. It matters to me, what you think."

He took a drink of his sweet tea and then cleared his throat.

"Sebastian's her *grandson*," I stressed. "It doesn't bother you that her blood runs through his veins?"

He studied me for a long moment in that calm way of his. "No. It doesn't. I watched him suffer at the hands of Athena for nights on end, watched him annihilate her minions and carry you to safety. It's actions that matter. Not the blood that runs through one's veins. Or the curse. Your mother taught me that. She was young, but she had the wisdom of an old soul. I only saw the danger she posed to the gods until she set me straight."

When he put it like that . . . I liked knowing my mother had changed him and made him a better person.

Our appetizer arrived. I picked up a fried calamari, my appetite returning. "I'm glad we did this."

"So am I. Once a week, dinner here, sound good to you?"

I chewed through my grin and nodded.

He tried to suppress a smile of his own, but it came anyway. He chuckled. My father was really good-looking, but when he smiled and that smile went all the way to his eyes, he was striking. That realization made me feel a little proprietary. I glanced around the restaurant and noticed not one, but two women casting glances his way. *Yeah, good luck with that, ladies. He's not interested. Not now, anyway.* I wanted him to be happy and not alone. But this was our time; our time to make up for the lost years and get to know each other.

"What makes you frown?" he asked.

I shook my head, "Nothing." I popped another calamari into my mouth.

My nervousness had disappeared, wiped away by what we shared, by a bond that was Eleni Selkirk, and the betrayals we'd both faced at the hands of the same two people. It always came back to Athena and Josephine.

"I met a witch. Out in the bayou." I proceeded to tell him the entire story, including everything I knew about the Hands of Zeus, and that the handless statue in Athena's temple was really the god himself frozen in stone. My father didn't seem surprised by any of it.

"Were you there when it all went down, when Athena went to war with Zeus?" I asked.

"No. It was before my time. My grandfather, however, was. I heard stories, tales of how Athena was in the old days. She cared about mankind, if you can believe it. All those myths they teach to humans about her were true. But like many old gods, she's changed since then. Slowly. Over millennia, she became jaded by mankind's greed and wars and vices. But she was still fundamentally good. Athena did have a child. Only her inner circle knew of this. My grandfather was her hunter at the time, so he was part of that circle. This was in the tenth century, right before the War of the Pantheons."

Our food arrived. I added a little hot sauce over my oyster plate as my father grabbed his burger and took a bite. I gestured for him to continue the story.

"Anesidora—Pandora, as legend calls her—prophesied that the child would one day bring down the king of the gods and start something called the Blood Wars. Word reached Zeus, and he did what he's always done: He protected his position. He took the child from Athena. That's what started the War of the Pantheons, which might be the same as the Blood Wars that Dora prophesied. Athena sent the gorgon after Zeus. Only it didn't go as expected, and her child was caught in the middle. They were both turned to stone."

"What happened after that? Do you know how the Hands got into the jar?"

"Dora. She disappeared with the Hands. It was the only thing she could do. She'd uttered the prophecy that damned Athena's child, making her enemy number one. Then she stole those Hands, which only added to Athena's grief."

"And the father? Do you know who he is?"

My father shook his head. "There aren't many who do."

"Melinoe said—"

His burger froze on the way to his mouth. "Mel was here? When?"

"Last night. After we got back from seeing the witch. She and Menai came to the house with a message. They confirmed that Athena lives, and she offered to lift my curse if I resurrect her child."

He set his burger on his plate, his expression going tight. It was clear he didn't like the goddess messing with me in any way. "Athena tested you, Ari. Before. Everything that has happened has been for this one purpose. She won't stop until she has her child. And she'll come for you to resurrect it whether you want to or not."

"Not if I'm curse free. Not if I can find a way to undo what Athena's done. Then I no longer fit into her plan. Game over."

"No. She won't let that happen. Remember, she will cover all the angles. She'll make sure your curse stays put until you've done what she needs you to do."

Every time I felt like I had an option, I hit a brick wall. My father was right. Athena would make damn sure I kept my power long enough to bring her child back to life. "So what do I do, then?"

"First, you need to possess the Hands." His eyes went hard and his tone even harder. "Then we strike our own kind of bargain."

I was struck by the "we" in his statement, by the fact that I had a father. One that was here, talking with me, eating a burger and fries. He was a part of my life and he loved me. A lump rose in my throat. I took a drink to wash down the emotions.

"Ready for dessert?" The waitress smiled at my father.

His gaze was on me, one eyebrow lifted as if to say he was up for it if I was.

"Sure," I said, "why not?"

EIGHT

THE NEXT DAY AT PRESBY WAS AN ODD ONE. I COULDN'T EXACTLY pinpoint why, but the mood was off. The teachers were quieter than usual and seemed distracted. None of the Novem heads—the ones who taught classes—were in attendance. Sebastian was nowhere to be found, again. And he hadn't been at the house this morning, making me wonder if he'd even come home the night before.

I spent each class growing more and more concerned, biding my time until I could meet with Michel and get back into the library. By the time my training session with Bran rolled around, I was itching to find out what was going on. Only he wasn't there. There was a note taped to the door, canceling training.

Something was definitely up. Hiking my pack over my

shoulder, I climbed to the third-floor administration offices to see if Michel was in his office. But when I cleared the landing, a heavily armed guard stepped into my path. Beyond his wide shoulders, I saw a row of guards barricading the hallway leading to the Novem's private study, where Anesidora's Jar was kept.

"You're not allowed up here."

"Uh. Yeah, I am."

"Not anymore, sweetheart."

Oh, how I objected to that name. I cocked my head. I hadn't gotten in my training time and was itching for a fight. But I needed more information, so I put on my innocent-girl face. "What happened? Is everyone okay?"

"Everyone is fine. This area is off-limits." His irises shifted from a murky blue to a bright blue, letting me know he wasn't human, letting me know he thought he could kick my ass. I knew even if I made it past him, I wouldn't get through the other six guys blocking my way.

"Can you at least tell me if Mr. Lamarliere is in his office? I was supposed to turn in a paper and . . ."

His brow lifted and his mouth dipped down as if to say, *Really, kid? You're going to keep trying?*

"Fine," I bit out.

My mind raced as I jogged down the stairs. The council had

to be protecting the library, which meant something had gone wrong. A break-in, maybe. I needed to find Michel, or Bran, or Sebastian. I slowed on the stairs, realizing I hadn't seen *any* of the Novem heirs today either. *Shit.* I hurried to the first floor and out the front door. What the hell had happened? The meeting last night was the only time all the heads and heirs had been together. And none of them had shown up today.

I sprinted past the cathedral and to the Cabildo building, which housed the Novem's administrative offices, only to find two guards blocking the entrance. I didn't even bother to ask. The Novem offices were on lockdown too. *Damn it.*

I ran to Michel's house and pounded on the main door. After a minute, one of Michel's servants who knew me finally answered. "Is Michel here? I have to talk to him. It's really important."

"No, he's not here." The servant stepped back and started to shut the door.

"Wait, what about Sebastian?"

"No, I'm sorry."

I let out a huff. "My father?" I swear if she said he wasn't in, I was going to hit something.

She stepped aside and allowed me to enter. Finally. "I know the way." I darted past her to the back of the house, out onto the large patio, then across the courtyard and garden to the cottage my father was currently calling home. I knocked quickly.

Relief flooded me when he answered the door.

"Dad." As soon as the word was out I realized—we both realized—it was the first time I'd called him that. It was as if time slowed down just to acknowledge the moment.

My father cleared his throat. His gaze sharpened, assessing. "What's wrong?"

"Something's happened with the council. They had a meeting last night. The heirs were invited. None of them—the heirs, the heads—are around. They weren't in class, the library is on lockdown, and the offices in the Cabildo are off-limits. Have you seen Michel?"

He and Michel weren't exactly the best of friends, considering my father had been an enemy of the Novem for so long. But Michel *had* lent him the cottage, and they were on speaking terms.

"I haven't. But if the library is off-limits, that means someone else is after the Hands."

"Yeah. Question is, did they get what they were after? The library is guarded like gangbusters."

I sat down on the bench in the garden and let my pack drop to the grass. "Could be one of Athena's minions. Or Menai and Melinoe could still be in the city. But that doesn't explain why the Novem have gone into hiding." Were they all inside in the

Cabildo? "I need to get inside their offices and find out what's going on."

My father crossed his arms over his chest. "There's always the full-on assault." Wasn't that just like a die-hard warrior? Suit up and attack head-on. I couldn't help but smile. "Smile all you want, daughter, but I have knocked down many heavily guarded doors in my time."

I didn't doubt that for a second. "As much fun as that sounds, I think we need a little more information first. But thanks for the offer."

"I'll talk to the staff and see when Michel was last home. Perhaps one of them can shed some light on where he's been."

I stood and picked up my bag, slinging it over my shoulder. "Thanks. I'll go by the Cabildo one more time and then hit the GD and see if Sebastian is there." This would have been a great time to have a working house phone at our place. A cell phone would have been even better, but the service outside the French Quarter was pretty much nonexistent.

My hopes were plummeting, and the fact that answers eluded me made me incredibly frustrated. I needed to get into that damn library, if someone hadn't already. My shot at the Hands might've just gone up in smoke, and I didn't even have the information to confirm or deny that possibility.

"See you later, then," I said, getting up to go, yet wanting to stay.

My father placed his hands on my shoulders. Then he gathered me close and hugged me.

He smelled nice, warm and safe, and my whole body relaxed. I let my head rest on his chest and closed my eyes, savoring the feeling like it was my last.

Eventually we broke apart. His big hands cupped my face as he gazed down at me. "My heart is yours. The hunter in me is yours. I am your right hand whenever you need me, and your father always. You are not alone." He kissed my forehead. "Not anymore."

Tears stung my eyes. He'd just cut right to the heart of it. All those old feelings of hurt and rejection welled within me, all those years alone, uncared for, abused, forgotten . . . they blazed through me like a fiery star that burned away into nothing. I was not alone.

My father leaned back, wiping my tears away. "Chin up now," he said softly. "Deep breath."

I rolled my eyes and laughed, swiping a hand across my cheeks.

"I will find out what I can. The Hands are not lost. Wherever they are, wherever they go, we will follow. I will not let another of my family fall to Athena's curse."

I nodded.

"Come now. That's the sorriest nod I've ever seen," he said gently. "Try it again with more conviction."

My heart gave a painful squeeze, and instead of nodding, I threw my arms around him and held on tight.

I walked the French Quarter, passing old storefronts, antique shops, gift shops, restaurants, and bars. Music drifted through the streets, mingling with the voices of locals and tourists. At one time there would have been the sound of cars, but now only service-related vehicles were permitted in the square since the Novem came to power.

I decided to head back to the square one more time before going home, walking to one of the long benches in front of the cathedral.

As I sat there people passed by, and the artists and musicians and fortune-tellers plied their trades. All the while, I kept my eye on the Cabildo and Presby. I was hoping to catch Michel or Bran leaving. A few people came and went, but no one I recognized.

I leaned forward, bracing my elbows on my knees and my chin in my hands, replaying the day's events. Eventually my thoughts shifted to my father. I barely knew him, but already I wanted to love him. Part of me already did. Getting to know him—and my mother through his memories—was something I had thought impossible. A dream.

I wanted to light a candle for my mother. All three of the

cathedral's doors, one main door and two smaller ones on either side, which symbolized the holy trinity, were open to the night air, and I could see the votive candles burning in the vestibule.

I picked up my bag to go inside, but a figure blocked my way.

I'd been so lost in thought I hadn't noticed Gabriel approach. He slid onto the bench next to me. He had an attitude the size of the Grand Canyon, but he was a Novem heir, so I sat, determined to find out where the hell everyone had been and what had happened last night. Gabriel leaned back, stretching out his legs and linking his hands over his stomach as his friends joined him on the bench.

Gabriel was powerful, and I hated to admit it, but he'd been able to glamour me twice now, which really pissed me off. I raised my brow at him, wondering what crap he was going to lay on me this time.

"Do you ever go anywhere without your groupies?" I asked, gesturing to Anne Hawthorne and Roger Mandeville, both next in line to take their places as heads of their family.

"They know a leader when they see one."

I laughed at that. God, he was arrogant. I couldn't believe that at one time—for a very *short* time—I'd found his sun-streaked hair, green eyes, and noble features attractive. Now he turned my stomach. "What do you want, Gabriel?"

He shrugged and stared at the church. "Just wondering if

you heard about our little messenger at last night's Council of Nine meeting."

Goose bumps rose along my skin. No. But I bet he was about to tell me. He smiled smugly at my silence. "Oh, this is rich. Bastian didn't tell you."

I was already stung by Sebastian's determination to face his problems alone, to leave me out of that part of his life, so Gabriel's comment hit its mark.

"Haven't seen him today," I answered. "Haven't seen any of you today. What's going on?"

Gabriel acted like I hadn't spoken. "You should really keep up with your boyfriend. We Bloodborns tend to *stray* to whatever looks . . . appetizing. Especially if that thing is a hot vampire with a body that won't quit. Just saying."

Anne Hawthorne let out a satisfied snort. She'd once had a thing for Sebastian—maybe she still did, who knew—and I wanted to sink a fist into that smug face of hers. Roger made eyes at me and laughed. Idiot.

"Is that the best you got?" I rolled my eyes, keeping a lid on my temper for once. "Get a life, Gabriel."

"I did. I got one about twenty minutes ago, and it was pretty damn tasty."

Gabriel leaned close to me. I tensed, steeling myself against his powers of persuasion. "If I were you, Clueless, I'd ask myself where your freak of a boyfriend was last night and all day today." His gaze traveled to my throat. "I don't know about you, but I bet his night was filled with sex and blood. Two cravings Bastian can no longer deny. He is what he is."

I swallowed, wanting to grab his neck and force my power all the way to his rotten heart. Gabriel got up and sauntered off, his friends laughing at my expense.

Anger pushed hard at me to go after him, to shove him to the ground and demand to know what had happened at last night's meeting. But I forced myself to stay still as he and his friends walked away. He was such an asshole. But a successful one in that he'd done what he set out to do—get under my skin.

NINE

I WAS TOO WORKED UP TO GO INTO THE CHURCH AFTER Gabriel's visit. It was hard to stop the questions echoing in my head. Sebastian could do whatever he wanted. I wasn't his keeper. And yet . . . What did Gabriel know that I did not? *Clueless.* Yeah, didn't like that word at all.

My anger wouldn't let me sit still, so I got up and headed home.

Another Mardi Gras parade was about to start, and Canal Street was filling with spectators. Before the Novem, crowds had swelled to crazy proportions during Mardi Gras. These days, with only the Quarter restored and able to host tourists, the crowds were still large, but not nearly as insane as in decades past. The Novem kept a tight rein on who came and went in their city.

Certain areas were off-limits, and travel was constantly monitored. Tourism was extremely lucrative, but it also came with its share of issues, since New 2's supernatural inhabitants weren't exactly keen on being known to the rest of the world.

The streetcar to the GD was nearly empty. I took a seat in the middle, slid next to the window, and watched the bright city lights fade into the semi-darkened streets of the Garden District.

I exited at my stop and then made my way down the dark street to the house. Before the house came into sight, I heard the furious beat of drums echoing through the neighborhood. Sebastian was home and he was playing hard and fast—this couldn't be good. *That makes two of us in a bad mood, then.* Sebastian worked out his emotions through playing, and tonight it sounded intense and angry.

I found Dub sitting on the floor in the living room with another pile of stolen grave goods spread across the coffee table. I passed the room with a wave, and then took the stairs two at a time.

In my room, I dumped my pack onto my bed, then stood there drawing in a deep breath and letting it out as the vibrations from the drums snaked through the flooring and into my feet.

Instead of hunting him down about the meeting and Gabriel's vague accusations, I sat and pulled off my shoes, lay back, tucked my hands behind my head, and listened to Sebastian's thunder.

He played for the next hour, the tempo eventually slowing until it stopped completely. I drifted somewhere between wakefulness and sleep. A door shut downstairs. Footsteps and muted voices came from below.

I sat up and undid the twist in my hair, raking my fingers down my scalp and through the strands. Basically putting off the inevitable. Now was as good a time as any to talk to Sebastian. But part of me was afraid of what I might hear.

I went down the hall. His door was shut. It was quiet. I stood there, torn between knocking and going back to my room. Instead I stepped to Violet's room, where hundreds of reflections spilled from her open door, painting the hallway with bright dots. I gave the door frame a light rap, sticking my head inside.

Violet's room was a surreal, magical place, filled with masks, beads, jewelry, and gowns. Piles of them lay on the floor, a few were on her bed, and some hung over her dresser and footboard. Masks hung on the walls and were stacked on top of the dresser and were looped over the posts on her bed. The light from the lamp bounced off thousands of rhinestones, crystals, and sequins.

In the center of a pile of gowns, a red mask pushed onto the top of her head, Violet sat, looking so tiny in the heaps of material. "Dub brought me a new dress." She lifted up a gauzy blue prom gown.

"It's pretty."

Her slim fingers played over the bodice. Pascal waddled out from under the dresses and padded to the small, plastic kiddie pool Violet had put in the corner of her room.

I sat on the floor, resting my back against her dresser, and drew in my legs. "The witch the other day . . . do you think he can lift my curse?"

Violet's expression turned pensive. Then she shrugged. "He thinks he can," she answered, as though that was all that mattered. If the River Witch thought he could, then he could, apparently.

I played with the hem of the blue gown. "Why did he say those things to you? About sacrifice and putting yourself in harm's way?"

She kept her gaze on the dress, fiddling with one of the rhinestones at the neckline. "He says that stuff all the time."

"What else does he say?"

She lifted her chin, her dark gaze looking so huge and fragile. "That I'm a treasure," she whispered. "The crowning jewel. A great, shining star. A diamond, black as night and tougher than the gods."

Shivers ran through me. Her answer was uttered with such . . . hope it made my heart hurt. I wondered how many times she'd heard those words, wondered if they'd sparked her obsession with building her own treasure, her own shining things. She wanted desperately to believe that she was valued and important. To me, she was.

"He's old," I commented after a moment, not wanting her to feel like this was an interrogation, but at the same time, I couldn't dismiss the River Witch's involvement in her life and his connection to Athena.

She nodded. "And he loves shiny things too. His treasure room is better than mine." She flipped the gown over. "Sometimes the zippers are stuck in the back or ripped. Then I have to fix them. This one is good, though."

The River Witch didn't strike me as one to like "the sparklies." But a greedy son of a bitch? Sure. In that way, he might be one of the greatest treasure hoarders alive. Who knew? "Where does he come from?"

"From the earth. Far away. I don't know. Where did you come from?"

"Memphis," I answered with a smile.

She thought about that and nodded.

"Violet?"

"Yes, Ari?"

"Do you know what you are?"

Her hands stilled and fell into the folds of the gown. Her throat worked as she swallowed. My breath held. Her eyes seemed to grow rounder as she stared at me. Her lips thinned. She shook her head, her bob swinging. "I don't know."

I reached over the gown and took her tiny hand. At my

touch she crawled over the material and into my lap, hugging me tightly. "I don't know," she whispered against my neck. The fear in her voice caused tears to prick my eyes. She didn't know and it frightened her.

She pulled my hair around her, nestling in the white shield as though it would protect her. "I'm a treasure," she assured herself, her voice the barest whisper. "The crowning jewel. A great, shining star. A diamond, black as night and tougher than the gods. Like you, Ari. Just like you ..."

"You *are* a star," I said, rocking her. "No matter what, you are the best of all the treasures in all the world."

Sometimes love took time to grow. Sometimes it came quicker, pinging you right between the eyes. The connection I felt with Violet was like that. She was right, too. In a lot of ways, we were the same. When I was her age, I hadn't known what I was either. I only knew that I was different, that a darkness lurked inside me.

"I love you, Violet."

Her voice was muffled. "I love you, too, Ari."

Black as night, Violet had said. I'd often felt that way, but now it wasn't a negative thing anymore. My darkness was a fierce thing, a strong thing, a powerful force that could kick ass and stand up to bullies like Athena.

As I held her, I stared up at the ceiling. Today had been

one emotional ride after another. *When it rains, it pours.* First my father and now Violet. And I still had a whole lot of unanswered questions.

I held Violet as long as she wanted, but it wasn't too long before she pulled away and crawled back under her pile of gowns. "See you in the morning," she said from under layers of fabric and netting. Pascal crawled from the pool, leaving a wet path behind him as he nosed his way beneath the gowns.

"See you in the morning." My legs were stiff as I rose and shuffled out, closing Violet's door behind me. Once in the hall, I didn't know if I had the emotional fortitude left to confront Sebastian.

But I didn't have to decide, because his door opened.

He stilled when he saw me standing there, my hand on Violet's doorknob. His hair was wet from the shower, face flushed, eyes bright. The hallway seemed to shrink with his presence. My breath grew shallow as all sorts of chaotic signals fired through my body. The instant reaction pissed me off. I gritted my teeth.

"Feel better?" I asked, the first thing that popped into my head.

"What?"

"Your drumming . . . Never mind." I bit the inside of my cheek, trying unsuccessfully to keep Gabriel's words from getting the best of me. "Were you with someone last night?"

His entire demeanor changed. He walked back into his

room. He hadn't shut the door in my face, so I followed him inside, closing the door behind me as he leaned his hip against the dresser.

I'd intended to ask him about the meeting with the council, but instead "Another vampire? Were you?" came out of my mouth.

Damn Gabriel! Damn me for my weakness, and damn Sebastian, because he wasn't even denying it.

"Is that where you were all last night and today?" I asked.

His eyes sparked and his mouth drew into a tight line, the agitation in him filling the room. He gave a short, disbelieving laugh, disappointment written all over his face. "You're really asking me that?"

"I am, and you know what? It pisses me off that I am. How would I know? You won't tell me anything. I have no idea when you feed, how you feed. . . . I'm in the dark, Sebastian. So, yeah, I'm asking."

"It is what I am now. I feed. I have to. And trust me, I like it a hell of a lot less than you do."

"Yeah, I hear it's terrible." I hated the sarcasm that leaped out, but I was unable to stop it. "Look," I said in a calmer voice, "I've learned enough to know feeding is some kind of high, a really good one. When you bit me . . ." Heat filled my face, and my pulse sped up. I know what I felt, and it was far from terrible.

"You can't tell me you didn't . . ." Enjoy it? Love it? But maybe I was wrong, maybe he'd had an entirely different reaction from me. And if that was the case, I was digging myself into one hell of an embarrassing hole.

Quiet filled the room; the memories of his bite were still so vivid. The way he'd held me pinned against the wall. His hot mouth on my neck. His tongue flicking out to lick, teeth piercing skin . . . I swallowed.

"Never mind. Just forget it." Why did I even go there? I should have kept walking right out of Violet's room and back to mine. I stepped to the door, but his hand slapped it shut. His body hovered behind mine, his hand staying braced on the door in front of me. Seconds passed. Then his other hand lifted a strand of my hair. A shiver went down my back. I let my fore-head fall against the door and closed my eyes, as a whirlwind of emotions swirled through me.

Sebastian moved closer and gathered my hair, draping all of it over one shoulder and baring the other. I went to turn toward him. "Don't," he commanded in a low voice.

My breath went shallow as he dipped his head and brushed a light kiss on my exposed shoulder, then my neck. His breath was so warm. My fingernails dug into the door as his lips trailed up my neck and to my ear. "I did like it," he murmured. "I loved it." His words sent tingles dancing along my nerves. "But it's a dark thing."

His hand closed around my hip. "I wanted to use you, take everything you had to give until I was satisfied. I almost killed you."

He turned me to face him. "I almost killed you," he repeated.

I wasn't sure how to respond to that. My heart pounded like one of his drums. "It was the first time," I said. "And look at the situation we were in. You were tortured and starved. That you were able to stop . . . with me . . . that says a lot. Aren't you getting better at control?"

He didn't answer.

"You wouldn't hurt me."

His forehead touched mine, and he shook his head. "I would. I'm only a couple of weeks old. I would."

"Do you feed from others?"

"I have. I am what I am. Accept it or not," he said defensively, "this part of me is not going to change.

"I want to accept you, but it's kind of hard when you haven't told me how you feel, what you need. How can I accept anything if you won't let me in, Sebastian? I don't know anything about it, when you need to feed, who you do it with, if you have feelings for that person when you do. . . . None of it."

He moved closer again, pressing his hips to mine, wrapping his arms around me. I couldn't hold in my feelings. "I don't like it. I feel like we were damned before we even began." I hated picturing him holding someone else, putting his mouth on their skin.

Granted, I got that he was afraid he'd lose control with me because I meant something to him. And yes, he was only a couple weeks old and playing it safe. He was a good guy, to worry about hurting me. But taking what he needed from others—I didn't have to like it. And I didn't understand why he couldn't open up and let me in.

Sebastian was the first guy I wanted to be in a relationship with. I hadn't known him all that long in the scheme of things, but we sort of made up for time in that we'd been through things most people would never go through in a thousand lifetimes. The horrors and triumphs we'd faced linked us. We had a strong bond. But our relationship was just beginning. We'd connected, and I'd wanted to see what would come of that connection. But where I was once hopeful, now I was not.

"I don't like it either, Ari. Just . . . let me work it out, okay?"

"Damn it." I pushed him away. "No, it's *not* okay. You want to touch me like this and I'm supposed to be okay with it after you've been holding someone else? I'm supposed to just agree with whatever you want while you keep me in the dark?" I jerked open the door. "Maybe I need to work out some things too, like whether or not that's *okay* with me. Oh, no wait. Don't need time to figure it out. It's *not* okay!"

I slammed the door, but it met his hand again as he followed me out of the room, ready to fight.

A horn blasted from outside.

Someone was laying on the car horn out front like it was nobody's business. Pretty sure it was Crank outside, I marched into my room to grab my weapons.

By the time I was done and downstairs, Sebastian was already walking out the front door. As I crossed the foyer, Henri and Dub's arguing carried from the kitchen—something about the proper way to chop potatoes.

Outside, Crank's truck was parked halfway up on the curb.

"About time!" she called, leaning out of the truck. "Hurry up, will you!"

I finished strapping my blade to my thigh and pushed through the gate.

"Get in. One of your teachers told me to come find you and bring you to the square."

"Bran?" I took a guess, lifting my hand to model his height. "Big guy . . ."

She popped a bubble with her gum and leaned her forearms on the huge steering wheel. "Yeah. Big dude. Brown hair. Nice tats."

I nodded. "Did he say what he wants?"

"Nope, but it sounded pretty urgent. So, he wants you to come. Like pronto."

I walked around to the open passenger side and got in.

Sebastian knelt in the empty space between our seats, holding on to them both for support. I wanted to tell him not to bother. Bran hadn't asked for him. But one glance told me he was coming whether I liked it or not.

As we sped out of the GD, Gabriel's words still mocked me, and my fists clenched. Next time I saw him, things were going to get ugly.

TEN

THE BRAKES SCREECHED AS THE TRUCK CAME TO A ROCKING stop in front of Jackson Brewery. "You want me to wait for you guys?"

"No," I answered, getting out. "You'd better head back home and stop Henri and Dub from killing each other."

She rolled her eyes. "They at it again?"

"Yeah. Something about chopping potatoes."

"Oh, Lord. Knives involved? Yup, I'd better get back. He's down there at 520-B."

After Crank left us in a cloud of exhaust, I crossed Decatur and started down St. Peter, the wide street between the Pontalba Apartments and the park of Jackson Square. Sebastian was a few steps in front of me, his shoulders hunched against the cool night air. The gnarled tree limbs stretched from the park over the street, and the late hour added a creepy quality to the night.

Sebastian stopped at one of the tall brown doors sandwiched between the ground-floor shops. He rang the buzzer to apartment B.

Footsteps thudded down the stairs. Heavy ones. The door opened and Bran's shadow loomed large. "About time."

"You're welcome," I responded in a tired tone. "What's going on?"

He lifted an eyebrow; I wasn't my usual snarky self. "The kid who lives upstairs has been sitting in the corner, speaking in tongues for the last two days. And seems your name's come up."

"My name," I repeated, surprised.

"Not your given name. She's mentioned your *other* name. God-killer. I think it's a message or some sort of prophetic warning. Come on, I want you to talk to her, see if you can figure out what she wants." Turning away, Bran muttered, "God knows, now that the shit has hit the fan, we can use all the help we can get. . . ."

I frowned, not understanding what he meant.

Bran led us inside the tall, narrow space, then up an equally narrow staircase to the second-floor apartments. He paused at the door marked *B*, looking a little stressed, which was very unlike him.

The apartment was pretty swanky. Jackson Square was lined on two sides by matching apartment buildings. They were known as some of the oldest apartments in North America, and home to many of the Novem families. High ceilings, heavy crown moldings, and expensive furniture—only the best for the Novem, while the rest of the population outside the French Quarter had to make do with spotty electricity and unsafe drinking water.

The instant we stepped inside, I was hit with a thick aura of tension and power. It raised the hairs on my arms and the back of my neck. In the living room, a couple sat on a couch, huddled together, holding hands, looking the very picture of concerned. Bran took the chair next to the couch and leaned close to them.

"I don't know about this," the mother said through tears, and I wasn't sure if her quick glance at me was one of fear or dislike. Probably both. It wasn't like I was going to hurt her kid or anything. I didn't even *want* to be there.

"We talked about this," the father said. "Whether it upsets Zoe or not, it might get a reaction, wake her up, something. We have to carry her to the bathroom and change her like a baby, Trish. This can't go on."

From the ensuing conversation, I learned that for two days Zoe had stayed in the corner of her room, facing the wall and rocking. She'd been uttering a language no one seemed to understand, mixed with a smattering of English and a few other languages.

One word had caught their attention: god-killer. And that had led them to confide in Bran, and Bran to summon me. Anxious to get the introduction over with, I cut into the conversation as Bran tried to convince the mother this was the right thing to do. "We're just going to go in and say hi." Sebastian and I headed down the hall before anyone could say otherwise.

As we approached the girl's bedroom, the air became thicker, the power so heavy it was like trudging through thick bayou mud. It made my heart beat faster, my head hurt, and my skin tingle.

"You ever see *The Exorcist*?" Sebastian asked from behind me.

"Why are you following me?" I shot back. "And Bran didn't say anything about demons." I stopped. "Please tell me there aren't demons."

"I don't think she's *possessed*. Not the way you're thinking."

"Gee, let's see, sitting in a corner, speaking in tongues. Sounds like possession to me."

The door was open. Inside, the space was how I'd always imagined a little girl's room should look. She was one of the lucky ones. She had a nice home, a family, and was cared for and loved.

Zoe sat cross-legged, her profile to us. Her back was straight, hands limp in her lap, and she was rocking slightly. Her hair was long down her back, a glossy black that needed washing. She wore pajama pants and a cami, and I pegged her about ten or eleven.

Sweat beaded at my hairline. I swallowed. It wasn't hot in the room, just . . . overwhelming. I met Sebastian's gaze, took a deep breath, then approached. She was a cute kid. Olive skin, open, unseeing, almond-shaped brown eyes.

Her mouth moved, the words too low to hear. I knelt down. "Zoe."

Nothing. Just rocking and soft words.

"Zoe. It's me. Ari." I took a steadying breath and said, "The god-killer."

The girl's head snapped in my direction so quickly it scared the daylights out of me. I recoiled, hitting the wall behind me. Sebastian took a step forward, but I signaled him to stay back. Her eyes didn't focus on me, but her words grew louder and faster. I was able to pick out some English. *God-killer. World. Tell her. Regret. Wake up. My child. My child. My child.*

Exhaustion was written in the dark shadows beneath Zoe's eyes. Her parents had a right to be worried. Whatever had ahold of their daughter was draining the little girl. And that ticked me off. I knew I wasn't talking to Zoe. And I decided the fastest way to get its attention was to piss it off.

I leaned forward, easily tapping into my anger from earlier. "Listen up, you parasite. Say whatever the hell you need to say and then leave the kid alone. I'm here. I'm waiting. You want to talk about the god-killer? Well, talk. Talk about me to my face.

Or do you always hide behind little kids? You too much of a coward, is that it?"

Sebastian winced at my theatrics. I shot him the bird, still mad at him. And, yeah, I was laying it on thick, but it was worth a try.

I'd barely finished the thought when Zoe's hand snatched my throat, shoving me back. Rising to her knees, she pinned me to the wall. *Holy shit.* Still, I stopped Sebastian with a hand. Zoe's head swiveled around slowly, letting him know she—or it—saw him. And then her attention returned to me.

Zoe leaned in close. The voice that came out of her small mouth was powerful and male. "Wake me. Wake me up. And I'll set you free."

Zoe released my throat and fell onto her back, arms straight out, eyes wide open on the ceiling as her parents hurried into the room and knelt by her side.

Sebastian crouched next to Zoe. She was still breathing. He turned to me. "You okay?"

"Yeah." I cleared my throat. "Fine. That kid has quite a grip."

"I don't think it was the kid."

Bran came in and leaned over Zoe, assessing the situation. Determining that she was fine, he nudged my foot with his boot. "On your feet, Selkirk."

"Thanks for the concern. I'm fine, by the way."

"Of course you are. You *are* my student. I don't train puss—"
He stopped himself in deference to the others in the room. I
couldn't help the smile that split my face. He rolled his eyes and
went to Zoe and her parents.

Sebastian held out a hand to help me, but I got to my feet
on my own. Zoe was sitting up and enveloped in parental love. I
was surprised to find I was trembling.

Zoe's eyes focused on me. Focusing was good. "You all right,
kid?" I asked.

She swallowed. "I'm sorry I hurt you."

I smiled. "It wasn't you. So you remember doing that?"

Bran crouched in front of her. "It's important that you
remember, Zoe. Anything at all will help us."

The mother smoothed Zoe's hair back from her forehead
and placed a kiss there. She wasn't letting go. The girl nodded.
"Okay."

Bran asked the million-dollar question. "Who was talking
through you?"

A pause followed, the words ringing in my head. *Wake me.*
Wake me up. And I'll set you free.

"The gods that sleep," she began, "they hear things from our
world . . . things about them and what they care about. Just bits
and pieces, fragments and whispers . . ." She shook her head and
then looked at me. "They know about you. The one . . . the one

who was in my head. He wanted you to come because you're strong. Your blood is strong enough to—"

"To wake him up."

"Yes."

"And if I do, he'll set me free."

"Free?" Bran asked.

"From my curse." It was the only thing I wanted to be free of. Or maybe that was god-speak for "I want to kill you." Because in a roundabout way, that would set me free too.

Bran turned back to Zoe. "Who was it? Who was he?"

She blinked hard. "I—I don't know. He kept saying weird things. Like poems or chanting. He's scary. He's angry and hurt—not physically, like betrayed hurt. He's . . . mad at himself, too, I think. He wants revenge. He has wanted that for as long as he's slept."

"Who?" I asked. "Who does he want to hurt?"

She thought for a moment. "It's not a person. It's a god. Athena, I think. I saw an image of her and another woman together. Like it was a memory he'd had. One lady was holding a baby, the other was smiling down at it, holding its hand."

"You ever see Athena before?" Sebastian asked.

"My parents did. And they told me what she looks like."

"At the Arnaud Ball," the mother explained. "Then again at the fight in Lafayette Cemetery, and later in the ruins when—"

She flicked a nervous glance at Sebastian. The ruins. When I changed Sebastian from stone to flesh, and he went nuclear on Athena's minions.

Bran reached out and ruffled the hair on Zoe's head. "You did good, kiddo. You stayed strong and you delivered a message from a god. Not many kids can say that, can they?"

When she smiled, Bran did too. Apparently, the Big Guy had a way with kids. Who knew?

"What did the other woman look like?" I asked.

"She has blond hair and is tall like Athena."

Another goddess, I thought while Bran rose and gestured toward the door. As I followed, Zoe captured my hand. "He doesn't want to hurt you," she said, trying to put into words what she'd felt from the god. "But he will if you get in his way. . . ."

"Thanks, Zoe. See you around."

Bran escorted us out of the apartment and back outside. The three of us walked across the street to the low stone wall topped by the iron fence that surrounded Jackson Square. I could feel the tension coming off Sebastian. He ran a hand down his face. "Just add this to the shit coming our way," he muttered.

"So you want to clue me in here?" I asked, trying not to grit my teeth. "Either of you? What the hell does this mean, and what the hell happened last night?"

Sebastian and Bran exchanged looks, but it was Sebastian

who spoke. "Athena sent a messenger to the council meeting last night. She made an offer. . . ."

Just like she had with me. Athena was playing both sides, covering her bases. "I'm almost afraid to ask. What kind of offer?"

"She wants the Hands of Zeus. She offered her immortality to the one who brings them to her."

"*Her* immortality?"

"Yeah. As in immortality plus all her powers."

It took a long moment for the implications to totally sink in. The paranormal world had all manner of creatures—many created by Athena herself. They lived long lives, some extraordinarily long, but they weren't immortal, not in the truest sense of the word, not like the gods—immortal unless killed by another god, or a god's weapon . . . or me. Athena's offer would set everyone on the trail of the Hands, making my job that much harder. But why would she highlight the Hands and let everyone know she wanted them?

Actually, it made sense. "She's ensuring the Hands will remain safe," I said. "If this many people know about the offer, it makes the Hands too valuable to destroy." And with the statue out of her control, she'd need to make sure it was safe.

And this little game changer made sure Josephine thought long and hard before doing something stupid, like destroying the statue because of some feud she had with Athena. Even

Josephine wouldn't be able to deny their value now.

But Athena was also ensuring her own mortality. Why would she do that? There had to be some kind of larger endgame, because I couldn't see Athena giving up her power. Unless—a nagging thought surfaced—she loved her kid so much that she'd give up everything. . . .

"And this new god," I said, glancing up at Zoe's apartment, "just adds more fuel to the fire. It's easy to put two and two together. A god wants to rise. He has his sights set on Athena. . . ." I paused. "He could be the father of her child."

"She'd anticipate the father coming into play, though," Bran said. "She'd know about the chatter, about what filters in to the gods who sleep. And I can tell you, she wouldn't mind one bit letting another god rise and destroy this city to get what he's after. Athena will pick up the pieces in the end and have exactly what she's wanted."

"If I wake this god and my curse is lifted, Athena loses. I won't be able to resurrect her child."

"Maybe. But this god might want you to resurrect the child as well. He might want exactly the same thing as Athena once he's awake."

They both come. The River Witch's words echoed in my head. Great. If this kid's mother and father were coming, Bran was right. We were screwed.

"How does one wake up a god?" Sebastian asked. "Why can't they wake themselves up?"

Bran shrugged. "Sleep means two different things to the gods. There's sleep as in rest, and then there's Sleep as in retiring from the mortal and godly planes. It's a choice made by very old gods, those who are tired and done with life. It is a decision that, once made, they cannot reverse themselves. They can only be revived from Sleep if they are woken, and the means to do so are a mystery to all but a few. Waking a god requires great power and comes with some serious consequences."

"Well," I said, thinking out loud, "maybe this god can help us. . . ."

Bran shot me a dark look. "Are you on meds, Selkirk? We're not waking a god. Did you hear what I said? We're talking *old* gods here. Primal gods. Supreme deities. The big dogs." He parked his hands on his hips and let out a heavy breath. "If this god wakes and has it out for Athena, it's gonna get messy. Trust me on that. The gods don't care who they hurt to get what they want."

"Speaking from experience?" I asked, thinking of Bran's descent from an old Celtic war god.

"My grandfather would slice open my belly and wear my entrails as a necklace if it got him what he wanted. And that's why I thank the heavens every night that he chose to Sleep. There's no way you're waking a god like that, Selkirk."

"A god like what? Who is it?"

He scrubbed a hand down his face. "Look, gods can only speak like that through their descendants. Otherwise the god would have spoken to you directly. Zoe and her family are just a handful of those left related to the Egyptian pantheon."

Sebastian let out a low whistle.

"Yeah," Bran agreed. "Waking an old Egyptian god equals huge fucking mistake. You need to find another way to end your curse," he said to me. "Because this way will mean the end for a lot of innocent people. We have enough problems with Athena. Her offer is going to make every power-hungry member of the council insane. And the news will leak, if it hasn't already, and then we'll have even more idiots to worry about."

"I hate to break it to you," Sebastian said, "but all the guards and the lockdown thing kind of waved a flag that something's up."

"I wasn't allowed on the third floor of Presby," I added. "The offices are off-limits—talk will start going around. Eventually someone will spill."

"Yeah, well, the exterior guards weren't my idea, but the majority vote won out on that one," Bran said.

"What about the library?"

"It's on lockdown until the council agrees what to do with the Hands. Until then, no one goes inside."

"So there was no break-in," I said, relieved. "A lockdown

only helps if the Hands are actually *in* the library."

I exchanged a glance with Sebastian. We were the only ones, besides the kids, who knew the Hands might be misplaced. Quickly, I filled Bran in on the fact that the Hands were either missing or hidden within the library. I told him that the Keeper was doing inventory to find them, and that we suspected Josephine of hiding them within the library or taking them.

"You might have told me this sooner," he said flatly. "Getting someone inside to see if the Keeper is done with inventory is going to be impossible now."

"Yeah," Sebastian said. "Already tried that last night. In the time it took me to leave the meeting, talk to Hunter, and get to the third floor, there were already guards posted."

"That's my job, Lamarliere," Bran said. "As soon as Athena's message was delivered, I texted my crew. They were inside the study, guarding the library before you and the other heirs left the meeting." He paused, shaking his head and looking disgusted by the events unfolding. "We should have sent Zaria's head back to Athena on a platter," he said gruffly, before waving us off and heading back into the apartment.

Cold slid into me. Zaria had been Athena's messenger.

I'd watched her drink Sebastian to the brink of death night after night in Athena's temple. I'd watched her tempt him with the blood of one servant after another. And I'd watched

Sebastian, changed and blood drunk, hanging with Zaria and Athena like they were old friends. Or more.

Numbness settled into my psyche. The wind blew in from the Mississippi, making the low oak branches that stretched over us creak.

"It was Zaria," I echoed with a sharp laugh. That's who Gabriel was talking about. During our entire conversation back at the house, Sebastian had neglected to mention her.

My throat stung. Did she have some hold over him? "Were you even *going* to tell me you saw her again?"

He didn't answer, and I wasn't sure if he knew the answer himself. He'd had several opportunities to confide in me, and he'd chosen not to. As though it was a secret. As though I wasn't part of his life. Well, to hell with that. To hell with him.

"I'm done," I muttered, shoving past him.

I felt his eyes on me as I marched away, part of me angry, part of me hurting like hell and wishing he'd say something, call me back, give me some kind of explanation. . . . But he never did.

ELEVEN

HE WATCHED HER WALK AWAY, HER LONG STRIDE EATING UP ground, widening the space between them. She hadn't gotten far, but it seemed like a canyon had opened up between them. His fists clenched at his sides, so tight his short fingernails cut into his palms. Every part of him screamed to go after her. But his body wouldn't move.

How could he make amends, open up, and explain?

Earlier in the day, he'd gone through his mother's things. And all he'd wanted to do afterward was drown out the memories, the hurt. . . . So he'd gone to his grandmother's to feed. For the first time since Athena's temple, he'd fed on a person and not a bag of blood. Had he been attracted to his donor? No. Had he wanted more from her than her blood? No. Well, maybe not before or after. But during, who could say? He wasn't sure. He'd been lost in a world of euphoria.

Afterward, it had felt so damn wrong. Anger and confusion sent him home to pound out his frustrations on the drums. He was losing his mind, losing his perspective, his understanding of right and wrong. . . .

Ari had gone pale at Zaria's name. Asshole that he was, he didn't elaborate on Zaria's appearance at the council meeting or how he felt about seeing her again. Maybe he wanted *Ari to see that he was different now. He wasn't the kind of guy she should be interested in at all. She was right before. She deserved better. Someone who embraced others, who needed others. It wasn't right to hold her, kiss her, or care about her—not when he was like this.*

How could she accept what he was, what he had to do to appear normal, and not like some goddamn animal? And yet a small voice told him he hadn't given her a choice. He was making it for her.

With a curse, he grabbed the iron bars behind him, wanting to rip them apart. When they groaned, he reared back. The iron bars were bent. He was so much stronger than he used to be. It was easy to forget that.

Shoving away from the bars, he decided to head over to Café Du Monde. Maybe a coffee would settle him.

The apartment building's main door opened.

Zoe stood there, holding on to the door, as though afraid to step outside. She glanced behind her nervously, and Sebastian knew she'd snuck down the stairs.

He waited.

"There's a message for you, too."

Goose bumps pricked his skin.

He crossed the street, every nerve leaping to life. She leaned in close, then glanced left and right before whispering, "Wake me up. Wake me up, and I'll set you free."

Zoe's words made the hairs on the back of his neck electric. A shudder went through him as she gave him one last look before darting back upstairs.

Twelve

I avoided everyone in the house when I got home. I threw my pack on my mattress and paced the room, wanting to take the vial of Athena's blood from my dresser and smash it against the wall. Instead I dropped to the floor, trying to work through my emotions with push-ups, then sit-ups and crunches, followed by lunges. For an hour, I worked my body. But I couldn't seem to turn off my brain no matter how hard I pushed myself. I was drenched with sweat and it still wasn't enough.

Aggravated, I changed into shorts, pulled on my sneakers, strapped on my blade and firearm, and headed out for a run. I'd run until I was too damn exhausted to think or care anymore.

I burned through several blocks before slowing to a steady

pace. Soon the constant strike of my feet on pavement and the rhythmic sound of my breathing were the only things I heard in my head. By the time I made it back to the house, my muscles were limp and shaky. After a long drink in the kitchen, I went upstairs, using the railing to pull myself up the steps, and into the shower.

After, I stared at the cracked mirror over the dresser, regarding my reflection in the aged glass. A solemn face peered back at me of a girl who didn't know what the hell she was doing. I tried to put Sebastian from my mind, pulled on my pajamas, and climbed into bed.

The next thing I knew, I was jerking awake to the sound of soft knocking. My door cracked open, light spilling inside as Crank stuck her head in. "You asleep?"

"No," I answered, sitting up and scooting back toward the headboard. "You can come in."

She left the door ajar so light could come in from the hallway, then came in and sat on the end of my bed, drawing her legs under her. A few seconds passed as she bit her lip, staring down at the blanket, seeming to struggle with her words. "So you're like a girl and everything. . . . Duh. Stating the obvious, Crank. I know you're a girl." She pulled her cabbie hat off and toyed with it. "What I mean is that you look like one."

"Okaaay." I had no idea what she was getting at.

"You're still tough, but you *look* like a girl. You look pretty."
She glanced at me. "I'm a girl. But I don't look pretty."

My heart gave a painful squeeze. "Crank . . ."

"I don't, okay? I'm always in these damn clothes, always have
grease and dirt all over." She flipped one of her braids. "I can
never do anything else with my hair. I don't want to look prissy,
but I want to look like a girl, you know?"

Violet came waltzing in wearing a gold half mask adorned
with a fringe of beads that hung over her cheeks and brushed
the tops of her lips. The beads swung against her skin as she
climbed onto the bed and settled next to me, her back against the
headboard and her legs straight out. "Continue," she said with a
regal wave.

Pink stained Crank's cheeks. Her slim fingers fiddled with
her hat. "So anyway . . . I want you to fix me."

"Fix you?" I blurted. "Crank . . . You don't need fixing. There
is nothing wrong with you."

"Just . . . can you do it?" She waved a hand at herself. "Make
all this better?"

Violet tilted her head to stare at me, waiting for my answer.

"Okay," I said. "You want to tell me why, though?"

I knew enough to know that this request hadn't come out
of the blue. Something had happened to make Crank notice
herself, and not feel good about what she saw. If someone had

said something mean to her, I swore I'd make them hurt. Bad.

"No," she answered.

"It's 'cause Dub likes this girl from the Marigny," Violet said.

"It is not!"

"She's thirteen, lives on Frenchmen Street above Spits's new shop, and has big boobs."

Crank gaped, her face turning beet red. "That is *not* true, Violet. I mean about him liking her," she said miserably. "She really does have big . . . you know."

I wanted to hug her. Sometimes it was easy to forget that under all that self-confidence and grit was a young girl named Jenna who'd lost her mother and father when she was little, and her brother a few years ago in the ruins. She had no one to look up to, to learn from. No guidance. No big sister to follow around, to steal her makeup and play in her closet. Crank was twelve, and I knew she was wondering why her body hadn't begun to change like this girl from the Marigny.

"Is anyone harassing you?" I had to ask. "Is this really about Dub?"

She gnawed on her bottom lip for a long moment before shooting Violet a glare. "No. And yes, but I swear to God if either of you say anything or act differently, I'll put motor oil in your stew and not fix anything around here for a month."

Violet placed her hand over her chest. "Promise."

"Me too," I said. "Motor oil tastes like crap."

They laughed.

"It's my birthday," Crank admitted quietly. "I'm thirteen today." She looked up and gave me an unhappy smile.

I hugged her, set her back, and said, "Well then, let the birthday makeover begin."

Violet jumped to her feet, exclaiming in delight that she'd be back with accessories, and then flew off the bed and out the door. Crank and I exchanged smiles. Then I got started. "The most important part of a makeover is to stay . . . you. You're a fixer, a driver, a hell of a mechanic, right? So we don't want to lose that, just change your look a little. If you end up liking it, great, but if you're more comfortable the way you were, then don't sweat it. Sometimes the most attractive thing about a person is that they're comfortable in their own skin. They own who they are, you know?"

Crank looked down at her stained overalls. "These *are* comfy. . . ."

"Then leave them. They're tough, and guys like a girl who can take care of herself. I bet whenever a guy sees you with a wrench in your hand, he's instantly intrigued. Like, who is that girl?

"So, some days maybe you lose the hat or do your hair different. Maybe add a little mascara if you want to go that route—just don't overdo it. Sometimes subtle changes are best. It'll make him want to figure out what you did differently. That can be more powerful than something glaringly obvious, you know?"

"I have mascara," Violet said, returning mid-exchange and dumping an armful of gowns on the bed. "I have a whole bunch of makeup in my room."

Crank wrinkled her nose at the gowns. "So not wearing those."

"They're not for you, silly," Violet said. "They're for me." And then she was off again, her tiny footsteps echoing down the hall.

"It would look cool to try some bracelets, a little bling," I suggested. "A nice contrast to the overalls. Something that says tough, but feminine, too."

Crank seemed excited and hopeful. I scooted closer to her. "First let's see what we have to work with here."

As I undid one of her braids, Violet came back, pulling a large cardboard box filled with makeup and scavenged jewelry. She climbed onto the mattress, out of breath and happy, and started undoing the second braid.

"I'll show you how to do a messy twist," I said. "That'll look pretty with your hair." And it would. Crank had beautiful wavy hair.

"I like those stick things you put in yours sometimes," she said. "Those kind of look girly and kick-ass."

I laughed. "Now you're talking."

I lay in the bed later, hands tucked behind my head, staring at the plaster medallion on the ceiling as I relived the makeover

Violet and I had just given Crank. Besides my last foster parents, I never had many ties to other kids or adults growing up. Being passed around from one foster home to another wasn't exactly bond-inspiring. Now it felt like I had a family, sisters, two unruly brothers, and a father who loved me.

And Sebastian . . . I didn't know what we were anymore.

I couldn't help but wonder if deep down, no matter what he said to the contrary, he harbored resentment for me. I was the one who'd made him take blood, who'd given him the first taste. He'd been drained and starved to the brink of death. And I couldn't watch him die. Of course, Athena had planned it all along, had put me in that cell with him, knowing the outcome.

But he'd never wanted my blood. He'd said he'd rather die.

Had our roles been reversed, I knew Sebastian never could have sat back and watched me die either. I pressed my palms to my eyelids, suddenly thinking of my mother and wishing like hell she were with me. I couldn't remember her face, her smell, her laugh, anything. I had a vision of her in my head, but I'd been so young when she left me that I didn't know if it was real or not. More like wishful thinking, a phantom I'd made up over the years.

A figment of my imagination. A ghost without a grave. My mother never had a proper funeral, thanks to Athena taking her body back to her temple.

Not liking the direction of my thoughts, I dressed and armed myself. Sleep wasn't coming to me anytime soon, so I might as well get some work done.

I sat in the living room for a while, cleaning my gun and letting my thoughts wander. The front door opened. I stilled, staring into the hall.

Henri appeared.

"Hey." I returned to my cleaning as he plopped onto the couch opposite me.

"Caught sight of your friends a little while ago," he said.

"Friends?" Most of my friends were upstairs sleeping.

"Yeah, you know, the hot hunter and the ghost?"

I raised my brow. "Menai and Mel are still in the city?"

"Looks like. I was doing a little recon around the square. Keeping tabs on Josephine for you, and I saw them on Presby's roof."

My pulse leaped. "They're zeroing in on the jar."

"From what I hear, Athena has everyone looking for it," Dub said, shuffling in with a yawn. "Overheard some big-time witch talking about it in Spits's shop." He slid into a chair and let his head fall back as though it was too heavy to hold up.

"Couldn't sleep?" I asked.

"Bad dreams. Lots of fire."

I returned the clip to my weapon and then shoved the gun in

the holster. I stood, wrapping the holster around my waist. "Too many people will be after the Hands now."

"Where are you going?" Henri asked.

The Hands are *my* golden ticket. I'm going to make sure Menai and Mel don't get them before I do."

Henri shot to his feet. "I'm going with."

Dub waved us away, letting his eyes close again. "You kids have fun."

THIRTEEN

WITH EVERY STEP WE TOOK TOWARD ST. CHARLES, MY MUSCLES screamed their soreness. I'd overdone it with my workout, but I didn't regret it. The emotional distance I'd gotten from it had helped immensely, even if I was paying for it now.

We caught the streetcar, and I found a bench by myself as Henri took the one across the aisle. I swiveled in my seat and asked him, "How's your side doing?"

"Aches sometimes, but it's getting better every day."

It was a miracle Henri hadn't been killed when Athena shot him and dumped him off the side of a cliff.

We rode in the rhythmic rocking of the car for a few moments.

"What's bugging you, *chère?*" Henri asked, his eyes sharp, brows drawn down, reminding me of the bird of prey he was.

How to answer? Everything was wrong, and a lot of things were right. Sharing wasn't usually my thing, but I found myself saying, "I just want this all to be over and done with, you know? I want . . ."

"What?"

"I want Sebastian to get better. I wish none of you had ever gone to Athena's temple."

"Yeah, well, you couldn't have stopped us. Bastian and I would have done anything to get Violet away from Athena. We *chose* to go. And we got Vi and your father back. Getting shot was a small price to pay to see her back home again."

I knew without a doubt that Sebastian felt the same.

"Sometimes you're a real hard-ass, Henri," I said. "And then you go and say shit that makes me like you."

A lopsided grin appeared on his face. "Girls say that to me all the time."

I shook my head at him, unable to keep from smiling back. But then I turned serious. "Why are you so hard on Dub all the time? I mean, I know he needs to control his gift and everything, but . . ."

Henri's smile died. "Dub reminds me of me at that age. I did a lot of stupid stuff. Got in a lot of trouble. I see him doing the same. I know the impulses, the recklessness, the energy. He doesn't think before he acts, and I don't want him to end up . . ."

Like him. But Henri couldn't say it. He looked at me with a depth I'd never seen before. "There is a reason I'm the only one left in my family. I don't want Dub to hurt the people he loves because he didn't take the time to think. . . ."

"Henri," I breathed, shocked and wanting to reach out to him. But what could one say to that?

He gave me a rueful smile. "I made my peace with my past. Now our Bastian, on the other hand—"

"Is struggling, I know. You didn't see him while you were in the Quarter, did you?"

"No, not this time."

My ears perked up at that. "But other times?"

Henri shrugged. I could tell he didn't want to break the bond of brotherhood he had with Sebastian, and I didn't want to force him to. He and Sebastian were friends long before I came into the picture. I wasn't going to put Henri in the middle. "Never mind. We're here." I got up as the car slowed to a stop at Canal Street.

We walked down to Chartres, which would take us directly in front of the school.

"I wonder if they're still around," he said as we closed in on our destination.

"We're about to find out. Can you do a few flybys of the school?"

"One is all I need."

"I'll wait for you on one of the benches in the square. Say five minutes?"

"I'll do it in four. Watch and learn, rookie. Watch and learn." Henri sauntered off, broke into a jog, then disappeared into the darkness.

Menai found me in three minutes.

Henri returned in four.

"Where's the other one?" he asked as he strode up to us, the ends of his flannel shirt flying behind him.

"Mel doesn't like the attention she attracts in the human realm," Menai answered casually. "She's . . . around."

"What do you mean, 'around'?" I asked.

"Mel's got one foot in the living world and one in the Under-world. She can go ghost whenever she wants. She could be here right now, and unless you're a seer or a powerful medium, you'd never know."

"No shit," Henri said, impressed.

"Why didn't you say anything about hunting the Hands?" I asked, crossing my arms over my chest.

"Look, I just delivered the message I was supposed to, down to the letter. That's what she wants, that's what I do."

"Yeah, right. Like Athena wanted you to help us escape her temple." It was getting hard to figure out what side Menai was on, and I was starting to think she was on whatever side benefited her own personal agenda, whatever that was.

"What Auntie doesn't know—and will *never* know," she warned, "won't hurt her. In this case, she knows what's up, so you need to get us the Hands, Ari."

I lifted my brow. Was she serious? "Isn't that what you've been trying to do?" If anyone should have success in hunting the Hands, it was the daughter of Artemis, goddess of the hunt. "But you don't have them. Why is that?"

"Because we can't get inside that stupid jar, that's why. Look, Anesidora's Jar prevents anyone of the Greek pantheon from entering it. It was one of Dora's spites against us. She and what's left of the Olympians are not on good terms."

"So you're waiting for someone to bring them out," I concluded.

Menai gave an innocent shrug. "You'd make all our lives a lot easier if you just found them and gave them back. What?" she said at my frown. "You're both getting what you want. Athena gets her child. You get to be free of your curse. I don't see the problem."

"Well, when you put it like that, neither do I," Henri said.

I glared at him. "Shut up, Henri."

"Why? She's right. If Athena is willing to make a blood-bound vow to turn you into a normal person, isn't that what you want? Or were you hoping to turn into a snake-headed monster at twenty-one?"

I got up from the bench. "No, that's not what I want. But neither of you are considering the repercussions of resurrecting that kid. What if it's not meant to be in the world? You can't just hand a child over to Athena without knowing who the father is. That kid was fated to kill Zeus, the *king* of the gods. What else will it be able to do?" Irritated, I shook my head. "I'm going for a walk."

Of course I wanted to be normal, to live a curse-free life. Right now my future was set, thanks to my curse. But if I could free myself, I could live past twenty-one as *me*—not some monster. Not hunted for being a threat to the gods. I wanted a future. To be with my family and friends. But no matter what anyone said, I knew it would never be that simple. I didn't even have the know-how to turn the child back to a living, breathing being. . . . And what if I failed? Then what? Athena goes nuts and kills me. End of story.

And even if I could, I just wasn't sure that turning over the Hands to Athena was the right thing to do. She had hurt so many people. She was unstable, manipulative, and psycho. Could I leave a child in her care and sleep at night?

But what if she loved that child? What if, despite everything she'd done, she'd be a good mother? Who was I to deny that child the wonder of growing up loved? I knew what it was like not to have that. And it was Athena who had taken my mother away from me.

I continued down the path, through the park gate, and onto St. Ann, heading past Presby. It was quiet this time of night, after midnight. A few late-night revelers wandered down from Bourbon Street, along with the occasional local and a few young pickpockets trolling the streets.

I stopped on the corner and looked up at the building that served as the Novem's elite school. The whine of a gate's hinges drew my attention to an alley that ran behind Presby and one of its satellite buildings. A figure slipped out the side gate. Shoulders hunched, tall, hands tucked into the front pockets of his pants. Yeah. That was Sebastian, all right.

I followed, wondering what he was up to, since all the stores and restaurants were closed or closing, and Bourbon Street wasn't exactly his kind of scene. But then the big gray mansion with the black iron balconies and tall black shutters came into view. Arnaud House.

I stopped across the street and watched from the shadows as Sebastian walked to the gate and let himself inside.

"You want me to spy?" The voice came out of nowhere, scaring me to death as a hazy form appeared. Melinoe.

"Let me guess," I gasped, holding my chest. "Your superpower is giving people heart attacks."

She shrugged. "It happens." Her eerie gaze returned to the house. "Your boyfriend was scoping the library."

"How do you know?"

"Watched him. Not much he can do. Guards everywhere . . ."

"Too bad you guys can't get into the jar. Athena would've had the Hands long ago."

"Not really. It took her a long time to find out where the jar was being kept, and even then she wasn't sure the Hands were inside."

"Dora sure did a number on Athena," I commented, remembering my father's words. "Making the prophecy known to Zeus, stealing the Hands, keeping them hidden all these years . . ."

"Hard to believe Dora and Athena were once like sisters," Mel said, in a quiet tone. "They had a near-unbreakable bond. Dora was Athena's first creation in the time of mankind's infancy. She was made with the help of Zeus and given life from the goddess's own blood. Dora was almost as powerful as her maker."

"Why would Dora share a prophecy she knew would get Athena's child killed?"

Mel shrugged. "Some say jealousy. Some say they fought over a male. Some say other things."

"You speak of her in the past tense. Is she dead?"

"No one has seen her or heard from her in a thousand years. To our pantheon, she died the moment she betrayed Athena." She nodded toward the house. "So you want to know what he's doing in there?"

Hell, yes, I do. It was on the tip of my tongue to say so, even though I already had a good idea of why he was there and what he was doing. But the words didn't come. I couldn't cross the line. No matter what happened between us, his life was his own, his privacy was his own—he'd made that very clear when he decided to shut me out.

"No."

"Suit yourself. You need to get us the Hands," she said, echoing Menai's same words.

"It would solve a lot of problems. . . ." But would it create more? I couldn't shake the feeling that it would. "Would Athena be a good mother, you think?"

Mel thought about it for a long moment. "Hard to know. The child was her first and last. When it came, she was . . . happy. She was in love with it, and terrified when Dora gave her prophecy. Athena tried to kill Dora for uttering those words. But once they were out, we all knew Zeus would never let the child live. Athena knew it too."

"And you can't say who the father is."

She gave me a narrow-eyed look. "No."

"What about Dora's prophecy? Is there any more to it? Athena's child was fated to kill Zeus and bring about the Blood Wars. It's all come to pass, hasn't it? Zeus is as good as gone, and the War of the Pantheons that followed—"

"No. The Blood Wars and the War of the Pantheons are two separate things. The Blood Wars have yet to come."

"But they will if this child lives," I guessed.

Mel shrugged. "Perhaps. You gonna wait here all night?"

I shot her a rueful smile.

"Suit yourself." She glided away, her physical body slowly fading until she completely vanished. Not a bad power to have.

Her words lingered in my head. None of what she'd told me was helpful in my gaining access to the Hands. I bit my lip, thinking. The library was off-limits for now. If I couldn't find information from the Keeper, then I'd have to get it from Josephine. Doing that, however, would prove a hell of a lot harder than chatting with an automaton. I stared at the house for a long time. A sense of foreboding settled into my gut and my curiosity burned a hole in my resolve. I wanted to know what Sebastian was doing inside Josephine's house. And more importantly, *why* he was shutting me out.

Finally I pushed off the wall and headed for home, leaving Sebastian behind and focusing on ways to make the vampire queen talk.

FOURTEEN

FOR THE FEW HOURS I WAS IN MY BED I'D TOSSED AND TURNED, unable to shut my mind off. And when it finally caved to exhaustion, my sleep was filled with images of the past that left me tired when I finally woke up.

I showered, blessing Crank for the hot water and knowing by the amount I had that I was the first to rise. The heat felt good on my skin. For a long time, I stayed under the spray. I'd come to the realization that despite the personal issues Sebastian and I were having, his abilities were essential in retrieving the Hands. I needed him.

Athena's offer had screwed things up royally. Had she left things alone, I would've been able to get inside the jar and into the library, no problem. Now I'd need Sebastian to trace me inside the Novem's study where the jar was kept—bypassing the security detail outside and the warded door, if such a thing was even possible. Once I was inside the jar, I'd talk to the Keeper. And then Josephine was next, and I needed Sebastian for that, too.

After my shower, I braided my hair and wrapped it into a low bun, then dressed quickly in a T-shirt and cargo pants before strapping on my gun and blade. I looked down the hall to Sebastian's door, drew in a steady breath, and went to see if he had come home.

He hadn't. No surprise.

After a quick biscuit grab in the kitchen, I left the house and caught the streetcar at St. Charles. I was the only passenger. The rocking motion on the tracks lulled me back into sleepiness. Before I knew it, I was at my stop on Canal Street. I walked quickly, trying to stir my blood and wake myself up, wondering what I would find today—Novem heads back at school? Armed guards still protecting the Cabildo?

When I got to the square, I knew immediately something was wrong.

A crowd had gathered across from the cathedral at the gate leading into the park. I edged closer as two people pushed ahead of me. One was Michel, the other Sebastian. The crowd parted for them and I saw another Novem head—Simon Baptiste—

amid several musicians, artists, and fortune-tellers who worked in front of the cathedral, and a few students from Presby.

I shouldered through the crowd. Blood made a trail along the stone. My pulse kicked up. A body lay sprawled on the steps.

Shock swept through me. Josephine Arnaud lay flat on her back, arms and legs out, one of her expensive high heels hanging off one foot, her hose ripped, her clothes covered in blood. Her head had been separated from her body and placed a few inches from her neck, as though someone had put it there to make a somewhat complete picture. Or maybe a statement. Her usually perfect bun was disheveled, and her face was sunken and white. It looked as though all the blood from her body had trailed down the steps and into the drain nearby.

The sight stole my breath. Josephine was *dead*. I glanced up and met a pair of emotionless gray eyes. Sebastian. He was pale, his dark lips set in a grim line. What the hell had happened in the few hours between when I'd seen him go into her house and now? A slight tremble went through me. Sebastian hated his grandmother, but there was no way he could have done this or taken part in it. Beside him, Michel knelt down and shook his head.

As the crowd grew larger, Simon gestured to a person next to him and handed him a phone. "Call Bran. Get security down here."

Michel got to his feet. While he and Josephine despised each other, he seemed worried and maybe even a little regretful at her passing. He put his arm around Sebastian's shoulder and squeezed. A kid tried to angle by me. I caught her shoulders and steered her back toward the cathedral. "Hey!" she said. "I want to see."

"Trust me, kid. You don't."

I ended up playing gatekeeper as more students arrived at Presby, but were then drawn to the scene. I noticed Sebastian doing the same as me to my right.

Bran appeared with several of his crew and started controlling the crowd and dealing with the scene. He posted several guards, then produced a sheet to place over the body. More Novem heads arrived along with many members of the Arnaud family, all looking pale and stunned by what had happened to their matriarch.

The bell rang and students were called into class.

The crowd thinned a bit, and I shifted to watch the crime-scene events play out as Sebastian came to stand next to me.

"I'm sorry," I said. "Do you know what happened?"

"No."

After a few seconds in silence, I told him what I knew. "I saw you leaving Presby last night and followed you to her house. What's going on, Sebastian?"

He let out a deep sigh and shook his head. "Come on." We

walked to one of the long benches and sat down. He leaned forward, his elbows on his knees, his hands linked as he stared down at the gray flagstones. "I go to her house to feed."

"But I thought your dad was helping you with that."

"He was. He was helping me, but . . . he doesn't understand. What it's like. What I need. How much I need it." He sat back and scrubbed both hands down his face. "It's like a drug, and I'm so far gone. . . . And for the record, I want to kill Zaria, not sleep with her, or feed from her, or whatever Gabriel told you."

Gabriel had mentioned sex and blood. The sex I didn't believe, but the blood, given Sebastian's secrecy, who the hell knew? "Look, I know what she did to you. I was there. But it's hard not to start questioning everything when I'm left in the dark," I muttered lamely.

As more Arnauds flocked to the scene, tensions rose. Wails and murmurs of disbelief filled the square. Several groups huddled together, some casting speculative glances Sebastian's way. He was her heir, after all.

Sebastian didn't seem to notice any of it. "They're going to fall apart now."

"What?"

"The Novem. They're already fracturing, taking sides. Athena's offer is too tempting. And now . . . Half of them already suspect my grandmother knew about the Hands way sooner than any of them did. They'll think whoever killed her did it to get information or the Hands themselves. They'll start pointing fingers at each other."

"Did you see Josephine last night?"

"She called me into her office and lectured me about family responsibility and traditions. But that was it." He paused. "I was able to go through some of my mother's things yesterday too." Before he'd come home and worn himself out playing the drums.

"Find anything?"

"Actually, yeah. Sometime before the War of the Pantheons, Josephine's grandfather was captured by Athena. The family never saw him again, so my guess is he didn't survive. The Arnauds have been sworn enemies of Athena ever since."

I remembered what the River Witch had said about Josephine and her family, about how her grandfather was instrumental in helping the Capetians rise to the French throne in the tenth century. The fact that Athena had captured and possibly—most probably—killed him was a good reason for Josephine to despise Athena.

"Who could've done that to her?" I asked, gesturing to the murder scene.

"I don't know. She was powerful. But no more than Simon or my father. Any one of the Novem could have done it if they lured her under false pretenses and struck her off guard."

"Your grandmother was smarter than that." I might have hated her for what she'd done to my mother and father, but I had to give her props—she was intelligent and extremely cunning. It suddenly occurred to me that my father had a very strong motive for ending Josephine's life. Her murder might not have had anything to do with the Hands.

But that notion seemed wrong somehow. He'd just started his life here and was getting to know me. I didn't want to believe he'd be willing to risk everything at this stage. But then, after what she did to my family, I couldn't really blame him if he'd confronted her and that's what happened.

Heated voices drew my attention. Michel and Simon were arguing. Bran put a hand on Michel's shoulder. The fracturing of the Novem was already starting.

"If someone does have the Hands now," Sebastian said, "and takes them to Athena, we're just exchanging one powerful psycho for another."

"No matter what she offered," I said, "I can't believe Athena would give up her powers. She has to be lying, setting a trap instead."

I leaned closer to him, dropping my voice. "Can you trace through walls and into the study?" I'd only ever seen him trace outside, never through anything.

"I've been practicing. Last night I was able to get inside the office next to the study."

"What about the wards?"

"Depends on where I go in, I think." He studied Presby. "I'm not sure, though."

"They're distracted," I said. "This might the only opportunity to see if the Hands are still inside the jar. . . ."

Then fear went through me. What if he tried tracing into Presby and couldn't, what if he slammed into the wall, or worse, got stuck in it? It'd kill him. Somehow I knew he was thinking the same. And then he was gone, a rush of air slapping me in the face.

Shit. I swung my gaze to Presby, heart leaping into my throat.

FIFTEEN

HIS BODY WENT LIGHT AS HE VANISHED. JUST ENERGY DIRECTED with thoughts that were still his. His father had told him there were very few beings who could trace like he did. So quickly, so easily. Disappearing and reappearing at will. But he hadn't mastered it yet. He might slam himself right into the stone walls of Presby. . . .

He'd do it for her, for Ari. To show her he was sorry, that he still cared.

In his mind's eye he saw the gray shadow of the school and pictured the small glass window on the third floor. If he hit, at least he'd crash through glass and not end up in a crumpled heap on the street below. He ended up in the study, his body solidifying in a blur of speed.

There were guards inside the room. Shit.

His entrance was so swift, at first they didn't notice him. But then two hulking demigods stepped toward him, and he blurted out the first thing that came to mind. "Wait."

He felt the power of persuasion course through him, the dark, poisonous gifts that made others obey him. He hated the feeling; it was so strong, too strong. Too malevolent.

One of the guards opened his mouth.

Sebastian cut him off. "Don't speak. Stay where you are until I say otherwise."

His entire body was amped up, vibrating. Shit. Okay. He was in. He'd done it. Now he needed to get Ari. He closed his eyes and willed himself away. And just like that, he was sitting next to her again. He grabbed her in his arms, concentrating on wrapping her with his power as they traced back into the study.

Once they were there and solid, he released Ari. She stumbled out of his hold. "Jesus!" Her body tensed as she saw the guards, her hand moving to grip her firearm.

"Come on," he said, grabbing her hand. "We should go."

Ari waved at the guards. They didn't even blink. "What did you do to them?"

"Just told them to wait."

They crossed the Persian rug to the ancient vase sitting in the corner. Anesidora's Jar was as tall as he was. It was made of clay, with sloping handles on either side. Symbols and writing had been stamped into the sides, and decorations had once been painted around its body, but many of those were only in traces now, just flecks of black and red color. The jar had a slim neck and a fat body that slimmed down again near the base.

A large, jagged crack ran from the neck to just above the base. It was a thick crack you could put your hand into, a deep space, black and eerie, and it always gave him the chills.

Ari wasted no time. She slipped her fingers into the crack. Light spilled around her fingers as she pried it open and stepped inside.

He drew in a deep breath and followed.

Darkness surrounded them. The jar was a vast dimension with no noticeable boundaries. Ahead, a faint light illuminated the long marble counter. It was quiet. "There's no music," he whispered. The Keeper always played opera on an old phonograph.

As they approached the counter, Sebastian heard the scratch and skip of a record player. Ari looked over her shoulder at him, concern written on her face, and then she jumped the counter and hurried down the long rows of study tables to the phonograph. She picked up the needle and set it aside.

"He's got to be here somewhere," she said.

The library spread out in never-ending rows, its shelves containing books, manuscripts, scrolls, statues, and treasures the outside world had never before seen. It was vast, and daunting, all surrounded by black empty space.

"I'll start at this end," he said. "Call if you find anything."

She nodded and took off, disappearing down a row. He started off, his steps echoing on the marble floor, the place taking on an eerie quality without the music.

As he looked for the Keeper, he thought of his grandmother, trying to fully process that she was gone. A handful of hours ago she'd been alive. She'd called him into her office and made some lofty speech about his future and family traditions. She'd had the nerve to demand he start attending mass with her at the cathedral. All Arnauds had attended St. Louis's since coming to the city in the 1770s. They always sat in the front pew, right in front of the flat stone that lay over the grave of Andres Almonester y Roxas. His grandmother hadn't let up, blackmailing him until he agreed. She'd loved the fact that he came to her home to feed. She loved the control it gave her over him. In her weird way, she loved him. For his power, for the pride it gave her that her grandson was the most powerful heir in the Novem.

Still, as much as he hated her constant maneuvering for power, as much as he'd tried to remove himself from her control, he always thought she'd be there, the bane of his existence. And now she wasn't.

And he wasn't sure how he felt about that. He was sad for her death, yes. Of course. Sad for his family.

"Sebastian!"

He raced to the aisle of study tables, looking down each row until he found her far down at the end of a row, on her knees.

He dropped down beside her. "Damn it." The Keeper had been destroyed. The tiny bronze plates that made up his "skin" were dented, the structural metal underneath them crushed at the chest, revealing bits and pieces of gears and mechanisms and wires. His legs were twisted beneath him, and his eyes, made of white stone inset with brown disks, were wide open and no longer sentient.

"It doesn't make sense," Ari said. "Why would anyone do this?"

But he knew why. They both knew why. The Keeper was an automaton. He wasn't designed to lie. Whoever had done this was covering the fact that they'd been here, had possibly stolen the Hands, or inquired about them.

"They didn't need to destroy him so completely," Ari whispered.

It seemed to Sebastian that whoever had done this had been pissed about not finding the Hands. He imagined that someone had pushed the Keeper to tell all he knew—who had been in the library, who had searched for the Hands—and the Keeper had paid for those answers.

"He didn't know, Sebastian. I asked him myself. He was confused that he couldn't find the Hands. His job was to keep everything in order, to be able to find whatever you needed. But he didn't know who moved or took the Hands. Do you think he can be fixed?"

Sebastian looked at the automaton. The damage was extensive. "I don't know." He took Ari's arm. "The Hands aren't here. We should go."

She got to her feet and gave one last regretful look at the Keeper. "We don't know that for sure. We need to find out if he finished his inventory." Then she hurried down the aisle to the marble counter, looking for any ledgers or books.

"He could have kept it all in his memory."

"But shouldn't there be a record? Unless someone took it." She threw open doors and rifled through the drawers beneath the countertop.

Light flashed in the darkness. The jagged crack where they'd entered looked so small and far away. And it began to elongate. Someone was coming.

Sebastian grabbed Ari and they raced to hide. As a dark figure swept into the light, they moved slowly into the darkness and toward the crack. Once they were back in the study, Sebastian whisked them away.

Thankfully, they appeared in the alley between the cathedral and Presby.

He glanced up at Presby, the view going fuzzy for a second as dizziness and nausea claimed him. Too much tracing could make him sick. "I have to go back."

"What?"

"Those guards. I can't leave them like that."

She clutched his arm. "You have no idea who else is in the study now, Sebastian. It's too dangerous."

She was right. But he had to go back. Whoever was in the library already knew he'd been there, because there weren't exactly a lot of people out there who could do what he'd done to those guards. They'd have figured it out. Regardless, had to go back, free the guards.

He leaned down, kissed her hard, and then disappeared.

Sixteen

Sebastian rejoined me seconds later. He was breathing hard, his expression dazed as though he was struggling to stay conscious. "Are you okay?"

"Okay." He glanced up and down the alley. "We have to get to my grandmother's house and look around before anyone else does."

He took my hand and we raced down St. Ann. He hadn't traced us there, which I guessed meant the tracing had taken a huge toll on his power.

We hurried through the gate to Arnaud House and down the alley to the courtyard. Two bodies, servants, lay contorted on the patio, blood pooled around them. His hand gripped mine tighter as we hurried into the house.

We were too late.

Inside, the scent of blood was so strong I could taste its tang in the back of my throat. It mingled with the faint smells of roses and furniture polish. My stomach shrank into a sour knot.

The house had been ripped apart. The broken bodies of servants, vampires, and human companions fell where they'd been slain. Not drained of blood, but struck down by brute force. Necks had been broken and spines snapped in half. In a blur of speed, one or two Bloodborn vamps or shifters could have taken out the staff in minutes. A sheen of sweat covered my skin. So much violence. Merciless violence. Whoever had done this deserved a slow, very painful kind of justice.

Sebastian and I didn't speak, not wanting to disturb the dead as we searched Josephine's destroyed office, then her private rooms, the bedroom, sitting room, and massive closet. Clothing lay strewn and ripped. Furniture busted. The pillows, bedspread, and mattress were torn apart, the foam and fillings in them all over the room like mounds of snow.

Josephine's safe had been broken into. Sebastian walked inside it, stepping over trays of jewels, old manuscripts, scrolls, and other priceless objects his grandmother had collected during her three hundred years. They'd all been left behind. Sebastian picked up a stack of three thin leather-bound journals.

"Might be something in here," he said quietly. My heart

went out to him. I could tell he was saddened and conflicted about Josephine's death. "I don't think she hid the Hands here. There's a reason she's lying dead in Jackson Square."

Because she wouldn't share the location of the Hands, and if she had, she hadn't given that info lightly.

"Who do you think did this?" I asked.

He swallowed, and I could tell he was just as shaken as I was. "Looks like a vampire or shifter kill. They both can be savage. But . . . there's no scent of them unless they had a witch with them to cover the smell. Could be all three working together. I don't know."

We searched the rest of the house. I kept hoping we'd find someone left alive, but everyone was dead. They never even had a fighting chance. Many had been struck down in obvious surprise—in the middle of cooking, cleaning the floors, reading the paper. . . .

There was no one to ask about Josephine, if she'd left the house, or if anyone had come to call. So how had Josephine gotten to the square? From the amount of blood at the scene, my guess was she'd been beheaded there. I wished I had a way to communicate with Mel. She might be able to help us piece together the last moments of all these lost lives.

An hour had passed since we'd arrived at the house. And we pretty much came up empty-handed. We were just leaving when a thundering knock echoed through the front of the house. I froze, exchanging a startled glance with Sebastian.

Slowly we eased down the steps and into the foyer. The doorknob rattled.

Sebastian peered through the peephole, and then said over his shoulder, "Simon Baptiste."

"Open the door," Simon commanded. "I can smell you in there."

We should have fled right then and kept our focus on the Hands, but Sebastian's jaw went tight and his eyes went angry, the gray turning to silver. He wanted a confrontation, revenge for all this carnage, and I knew this would not end well.

Sebastian handed me the journals, then opened the door. His shoulders filled the doorway, his posture confident and pissed off.

Standing with Simon were two other Novem heads, Soren Mandeville and Katherine Sinclair, and a large gathering of their families. Simon gave me the creeps; his bearing pompous and malevolent. Brutality clung to him; it was in the cunning and anticipation lurking behind a classically handsome face. The arrogance in his eyes reminded me of Gabriel, and I knew one day Gabriel would be just like his father, bloated on his power and sure in his right to lord it over others.

"Your being here is . . . suspect," Simon said.

"Why should it be?" Sebastian fired back. "We found the house destroyed and everyone in it dead. But then"—his gaze went to each of the Novem leaders—"I'm guessing at least one of you, or all three, already knows that."

Simon's eyes narrowed, and he stood straighter. "You *dare* accuse us?"

Sebastian crossed his arms over his chest. "Seeing as the three of you are here, probably wanting to find the Hands yourselves, yeah, I am."

"We're *here* to investigate her murder," Katherine Sinclair chimed in.

"Sure you are. Who nominated you head of security? Bran should be here."

"Bran *is* here," a deep voice said in the hallway behind us.

Relief rushed over me as I turned to see my father, Bran, Michel, and Rowen, followed by several members of their families. They must have come through the back like Sebastian and I had.

Bran and Michel moved past me to stand behind Sebastian.

"So it comes to this," Simon intoned.

"No one has to draw lines in the sand," Bran said. "We all know discord is what Athena's after. You're playing right into the goddess's hands. You know better."

"Or maybe this has been a long time coming." Simon's

gaze flicked to Sebastian. "We have every right to make sure Josephine did not take the Hands from the library. Her behavior and actions have been in question since the battle in the ruins."

"And it's my job to deal with it," Bran fired back. "You don't see me coming to your office and sticking my nose in tourism, electricity, banking. This is *my* territory."

"There is too much at stake," Soren said, "to leave the inquiry into Josephine's death to one person."

"The only thing at stake is us splintering," Michel stressed. "And if that happens, it's all on you three. Will you ruin everything we have worked for and put this city in turmoil to have a chance at the Hands and immortality? The three of you will turn against each other as you turn against us now."

A small flutter caught my attention. A faint electrical zing and high-pitched squeals, so tiny and faint, yet somehow . . . familiar. I scanned the crowd gathered behind the Novem heads, seeing traces of small light trails dart from person to person. *What the hell?*

The crowd stirred.

Names and accusations flew. Magic built and teeth elongated. The time for talking was over. My father pulled me away from the door and shoved me down as the front windows exploded, raining shards of glass on our heads. The journals spilled from my hands.

I withdrew my firearm as Sebastian and the others surged out the front door and into the street. Blood and grunts and screams filled the air. I crept to the busted-out window. There was another group of shifters and witches closing in on Simon and his entourage from the side street. Ramseys and Deschanels. Hawthornes and Lamarlieres. They were on our side, the Cromleys apparently staying out of the fight.

Flashes of magic lit the night. Bran wielded his huge broadsword. Michel drew energy into his hands and let it loose at a vicious-looking vampire. I took shots through the window. My father, with a borrowed blade, sliced through any and all comers near my position.

I searched for Sebastian but couldn't find him in the melee. I jumped through the window, meeting my first attacker and emptying the last of my bullets into him. I switched to my blade, my adrenaline pumping like crazy as a large mangy bear slid to a stop in front of me. It rose up on its hind legs and let out a roar that blew the hair back from my face. My blade seemed woefully inadequate, and the bad thing about my power? I had to get close to use it.

The bear lunged. I feigned right, but wasn't quick enough. Its shoulder bumped mine and sent me flying, the blade knocked from my hand. The bear whirled around as I got to my feet, already calling my power, waking the serpent. The bear charged again, and this time I stayed still. I couldn't jump over it, and if I waited too long, those claws would dig deep.

It was closing in fast. I ran toward it, arms pumping. Almost there. I executed a slide, gliding on the shards of glass littering the street, and went through its front legs. It came over me. I grabbed the bear under the jaw. As soon as my hand touched fur, the fur went hard, the change spreading over it, turning fur, skin, flesh, and bone into stone. I rolled before it dropped and crushed me.

As I got to my feet, I was hit immediately in the gut by a shoulder. The force sent me airborne. I landed hard, the back of my head cracking on pavement. Hot pain arced over my skull. Stars danced in my vision. *Jesus.* I pushed up, dazed. *Focus, damn it!*

The vamp stalked me slowly as though he had all the time in the world. He wanted me to know who he was. Gabriel. He'd been waiting for this a long time, and his sadistic smile told me he was going to enjoy taking me apart. *Same here,* I thought.

Slowly I got up. Pain thumped through my head in time with my pulse. Gabriel stopped in front of me, a thin smile on his lips and a fanatical spark in his eyes. Yeah. Like father, like son.

"What's wrong, Gabriel," I managed, "too chickenshit to take me?"

We circled each other. I kept a firm block on my mind to keep him from glamouring me. I focused on the gruesome images of what had been done to Josephine and her staff. Someone like Gabriel could've done that without breaking a sweat.

"I'll enjoy draining you, freak."

"To do that you'll have to get close, Gabriel. Real close. Stone-cold close." I put my hands under my armpits and squawked at him, knowing Crank would be proud, knowing it would drive Gabriel over the edge. He lunged.

The moment he touched me, the serpent in me struck, leaping to life with such ferocity that it left me momentarily stunned. He thought he was quicker, thought he could sink his fangs into my flesh before my power could stop him. He was wrong.

My fingers clutched his wrists as his hands wrapped around my throat, squeezing and trying to bend my head sideways to snap my neck. But they were already cold and hard. He stared at me in shock, frozen, our faces so close. So intimate. He began to choke. The skin at his throat went white, like a million microscopic marble bugs scrambling upward and leaving stone in their wake. The choking stopped as his vocal cords hardened.

Up over his chin, his open mouth, his wide, shocked eyes and finally his head and then ... nothing.

My pulse thundered in my ears. I was trapped in the grip of a several-hundred-pound statue. I pulled at Gabriel's hands. I'd had no other choice but to turn him. Too bad he'd been at my throat when that happened. A glance over my shoulder showed me another vampire was incoming.

And it was Simon, his eyes blazing with murderous intent. Oh God. I'd just killed his son.

I struggled, the statue's hold so tight I was unable to get out more than a few faint screams. But it was enough. Michel and Bran tackled Simon from behind, and the fight was brutal. Simon cared for nothing except getting them off him so he could kill me. He was a maniac in his grief, managing to send Bran flying through a second-floor window, then dragging Michel behind him, refusing to stop, refusing to break his stride as he came for me.

If I could topple the statue, maybe the arms would break and I could run. I rocked to my left and right. Simon shouted in horror, seeing what I was doing, knowing that if I succeeded, Gabriel was gone for good. He shoved Michel off and rushed me in a blur of supernatural speed.

But I was already falling. Gabriel and I crashed to the ground to the sound of his father's roar. One stone arm broke at the elbow, the other at the wrist. I scrambled back, the hands still attached around my neck as Simon plowed into me. We rolled. One marble hand was wrenched free in the roll. Simon ended up on top of me. He wrenched the other marble hand free, raising it high over my head. He was going to bludgeon me to death.

For a second, shock got the best of me.

Then a hand grabbed on to the stone arm and held it still.

A Son of Perseus was a terrifying thing if you were in his sights. My father's face was hard and grim as he pitted his strength against Simon's. His other hand went to shove his knife into Simon's throat when Mandeville appeared at my father's side, a blade pressed between his ribs. My father was still going to do it, to save me, but I shook my head. Mandeville would shove that blade straight through his ribs and into his heart, and I had no idea if that blade had the power to end my father's life or not.

Simon's eyes burned with hatred. "You took someone I love," he sneered at me, voice trembling. "I will do the same. Go to her house," he told Mandeville. "Search it for any sign of the Hands. Kill anyone inside."

"No!" I struggled, but he pinned me with the stone arm as Mandeville released my father and disappeared in a haze of speed.

My father made a move to slice Simon's throat, but Simon dropped the marble arm and caught my father's hand in the blink of an eye, stilling the blade before it could sink deep enough to kill. Simon hissed at me, "This isn't over. Say good-bye to your friends."

In a blur, he was gone. My father collapsed over me, his hands hitting the pavement. He pushed himself back up as Sebastian appeared like a demon from hell, taking out a shifter lunging in midair right for us.

Jesus.

I scrambled up, shaking, as the shifter went flying into the building across the street. "The kids," I told him, the terror sinking in. "Simon and Mandeville, they've gone to the GD."

Sebastian grabbed me and we traced, landing in a tumble in the middle of First Street as his power gave out. His head hung low and he was shaking, but he pushed to his feet. I caught his hand and together we ran the rest of the way, hoping like hell Simon and Soren Mandeville hadn't beaten us to the house. Hoping like hell the kids weren't home.

Please, don't let them be home.

My lungs burned. My muscles hurt so bad I wasn't sure how I stayed on my feet. An orange glow bled through the trees. It grew the closer we came, and I heard the distinct crackle of fire.

Oh God. The house was burning.

I drew up short in the street out front. The sound of things being smashed inside echoed over the inferno. Heart lodged in my throat, I ran for the house, but Sebastian held me back. "No."

A figure burst through the front door, engulfed in flames. Not one of the kids. A vampire.

"And stay out!" Dub stepped through the flames, following.

The burning vampire staggered across the pavement and collapsed in the middle of the road.

A faint moan from across the street drew my attention. *No.* Crank's truck lay upside down in a dented heap, against the neighboring fence. I raced over, shouting her name, dimly aware of Sebastian beside me, of Dub calling her name, and the intense heat he brought with him.

I dropped to my knees at the driver's-side door, which was now only a few inches off the ground. It was enough for me to see the seat was empty. She hadn't been wearing her belt. "Crank! Jenna!" Movement caught my eye. Her foot was stuck in the passenger-seat crease. She was sandwiched somewhere between the fronts seats.

"Crank! Hold on, we're coming!"

Metal creaked and moaned as Dub crawled into the passenger side and eased down into the mangled mess. He braced his feet on the dash and front seat, bending down to search for Crank.

"Is she okay?" He didn't answer. "Damn it, Dub," I choked out, my voice shaking, "is she okay?"

She *had* to be okay.

SEVENTEEN

MICHEL ARRIVED AS WE TRIED TO GET CRANK OUT OF THE mail truck. She wasn't responding. Sebastian shoved the back door down and climbed inside. I went in after him, catching a glimpse of Crank on her side, one leg bent at an unnatural angle and her arms wrapped around her middle.

No matter how many times we said her name, she didn't respond.

"We shouldn't move her," I said, worried something might be broken in her spine or neck. "Can you tell what's wrong?" There were too many mail bags for me to angle my way next to him and see her completely.

He shook his head. "But it looks bad."

Dub paced behind the truck. Michel leaned in. "I can stabilize her. We need to get her to a hospital. Was there anyone else in the house?"

My stomach dropped. We scooted out of the truck and I stared at Dub. Behind us, 1331 blazed, the heat coming off it hitting us like a hell-born wind. All the rotting wood, the furniture, the weeds and overgrowth had gone up like kindling. "Dub, where's Violet and Henri?"

He kept pacing and biting his nails, his wide eyes on the ground but unseeing.

"Dub!" I stepped in his path and placed my hands on his shoulders. He stopped but wouldn't look at me. He was burning up; even his clothes were hot to the touch. Emotion poured off him. I whispered his name, and finally he lifted his chin, his face cracking with horror and grief. "I didn't mean it. They came and I just . . ."

"Hey. It's all right. You did good. You did what you had to do. Where are the others?"

"I don't know. They weren't home. But Crank, she . . . She was pulling up, and one of them just stepped in front of her truck and stopped it like it was nothing and then he—he threw it across the road and came inside."

Tears streamed down his face, and I hugged him to me. "It's okay. She'll be okay."

He stepped back and swiped his hand under his nose and

sniffed hard, nodding like he was trying to convince himself.

Michel pulled Crank from the truck. While she was in his arms, her body stayed frozen just the way we'd found her. Michel must've used his magic to keep her body still. "I'll take her to Charity Hospital," he said, and then he was gone, leaving us there alone to stare at our house being eaten up by fire.

"Who were they?" Dub asked.

A heavy weight settled on my shoulder. I'd killed Gabriel, and Simon had exacted his revenge.

"It was—" Sebastian spoke up.

"It was me," I cut in. "I killed one of the Novem's heirs, and his father came here to get back at me."

Dub went still and his eyes met mine. They were blank, taking in the news, letting it sink into his bones.

I'm sorry. I'm so sorry.

"My grandmother is dead. The Novem is at war," Sebastian said over the apology echoing in my head. "They're all after the Hands now."

Dub blinked, his face going a little paler than before. "And we're stuck in the middle," he echoed in a hollow tone. Anger twisted his features. "She's human, you know!" He threw out his hand toward the truck. "She's not like us! She can't stand against them."

He was right. Crank couldn't protect herself, or outrun a

supernatural. She was smart and brave, and could hold her own for a little while, but facing down a vampire, shifter, or powerful witch—not to mention facing a bunch of them . . .

"This shouldn't have happened," Dub said through tears. "This shouldn't have happened!"

He pushed past us and ran down the street. I watched his image fade into the darkness, my chest feeling as though it burned as hot as the three-story fire beside us. I wiped at my tears, angry with myself, angry that I hadn't been here, that I'd caused this.

And Dub. Poor Dub was left to defend himself. He was just a kid too. Just a fucking kid.

"Hey." Sebastian spun me around to face him. "Don't do this to yourself."

"Why not? It's my fight, and I brought all of you into it."

"You didn't murder my grandmother," he said. "You didn't set the Novem up to fracture. You didn't make Gabriel attack you. So don't do that. Don't take on all the blame. Don't start feeling sorry for yourself."

I flinched as though he'd slapped me and stepped back, caught off guard by his words. Sorry for myself? Is that what he thought? That I only cared about me?

"Wait," he started, shaking his head, frustrated. "That's not how I meant it."

"Go to hell," I said through tears, walking away and then

turning back. "I feel sorry for them, for what my being here has caused. I can feel that. I'm allowed because I *care* about them. Tell you what," I said, swallowing my grief. "You knock off the 'lying to my face and shutting me out' routine and then maybe you'll have the right to say what you just did."

I swung around, intending to march off, but ran smack into Henri. He stilled me with his hands on my arms. I let my forehead fall against his chest, wanting to let all the fear, worry, and anger out, but I forced it down and moved away.

Henri's gaze was riveted on the house. It was completely engulfed now. Behind him I saw movement, a shadow down the street, crossing into the swath of light from the streetlamp.

It was the River Witch in his cloak and hood walking with a cane, and a tiny girl holding his hand. Relief weakened my legs. Thank God. Violet was okay. I hugged Henri. He let out a surprised grunt. And then I was running.

I dropped to my knees in front of Violet and hugged her.

When I released her, she stared at me for a long moment, her face expressionless, but her dark eyes were filled with regret. "The house is on fire," she said. "All my treasures are burning."

"I know," I said. "I'm sorry."

My mother's letter and the few things she had left for me were burning too. I stood and watched the flames lick the sky. The house next door would catch fire soon. Sparks had already lit the trees between the two houses. The entire GD might go up in flames.

"Feels good," the River Witch remarked, "the heat on my face . . ."

I was surprised to see him out of the bayou. "What are you doing here?"

The gaze he fixed on me was bright and more than just intelligent; it was cunning and almost . . . pleased. "I've come to help you, child. Things are at work that you cannot overcome on your own, things that need to be . . . monitored."

I frowned at his odd choice of words. Suspicion had lingered with me from our first meeting. "Why help at all? What do you care?"

"Because the alternative, if you should lose, is unacceptable." He tapped his cane on the ground. "Now come, let's see what we can do about this fire, shall we?"

As Violet went to see Sebastian and Henri, the witch moved to the middle of the street, which was as close as one could get to the flames now. There were a few fire stations and EMTs in the French Quarter, mostly to deal with the human tourists and locals. No one was going to come to our rescue out in the GD. And even if they did, there was no way they'd stop the inferno.

Bran showed up, bruised and bloodied, his sword hung over

his back like he'd just stepped off some ancient battlefield. He took quick stock of the situation. "Where's Michel? We need him back in the Quarter."

"He took Crank to the hospital." I nodded to the truck. "She was inside."

A hard glint came into his eyes. "Bastard. And Simon?"

"I'm not sure. He's either burning or gone."

"Things are going to get worse, Selkirk. Athena has used a simple divide-and-conquer strategy. Phase one is complete; we're divided. Conquer is next. She'll launch her own offensive soon. United, we could have stood against her. We've done so in the past. Divided, we won't stand a chance."

The witch lifted his hands, and the roaring fire picked up. The flames began to swirl around like a tornado, lifting higher into the air as though a giant vacuum was pulling the flames from the house until finally they dissipated into the sky, leaving behind a smoking, charred skeleton.

My father appeared by my side. I glanced over at him, relieved that he was okay. His hand gripped my shoulder and squeezed, and I could see he was feeling the same as me.

"How long do you think we have before she comes?" I asked him as Sebastian, Henri, and Violet joined us.

"She'll give the Novem time to self-destruct, but not enough time to risk them coming back together. A day or two at most."

"Simon and the others, they'll destroy everything. Even the jar," Sebastian said.

"They won't find the jar," Bran said.

Surprised, I asked, "What do you mean?"

"It means I got it the hell out of Presby right after your little visit. That jar contains vast amounts of our combined knowledge. I'll be damned if they destroy it looking for Athena's kid."

So it had been Bran who'd opened the crack in the jar as we'd knelt with the Keeper.

"How'd you manage that?" my father asked, impressed. From the tone, it sounded like moving the jar was a considerable feat.

"With a little help from Rowen. We can thank the gods that witch is on our side, because her power is unlike anything I've seen."

The River Witch shuffled over to us.

Bran's eyes narrowed and my father's became suspicious. "Who the hell are you?" Bran demanded.

The witch regarded him with disinterest, obviously not impressed. "They call me the River Witch. I live out in the bayou. I see things, many things. I am powerful." He tipped his head slowly toward the burned-out shell that had once been our home as evidence of his power. "I have lived in the bayou since before the first settlers arrived. This is my home, and I won't see it destroyed."

Bran let out a *humph* and looked beyond the witch to my father, the impatience in him clear. "You up for helping me keep the peace, hunter?"

"I could use the exercise. But my sword is with Ari."

I dipped my head, telling him how much his loyalty meant to me. "You might as well go," I said. "I'm heading to the hospital to check on Crank."

He nodded. "If you need us . . ."

"I'll know where to find you." All I had to do was look for the bloodshed. Between my father and Bran, things were going to get even messier.

After they left, the rest of us made our way to Charity Hospital. It was on the upper boundary between the French Quarter and the ruins, and close to Canal Street, which formed the western border of the Quarter.

We found Michel at the desk in the emergency room. "They're inserting a chest tube to inflate her lung and setting a broken leg. A few other bumps and bruises to look over, but she should recover."

Henri swore softly.

Michel gestured to the waiting room. "Your young friend is in there."

We joined Dub in the waiting room, Michel leaving to deal with the fighting. The mood was somber as we found seats and waited. I felt a stare and found Sebastian's gaze on me. I thought of his words earlier. Damn right I was feeling sorry. Crank was in the hospital, for God's sake. How could I not feel responsible? Whatever. A second later he was standing in front of me.

"Can I talk to you?" He motioned for us to go out of the room.

We went down the hall, finding a quiet corner. "What I said . . . It came out wrong before." He dragged a hand down his face with a loud sigh. "The girl. Zoe."

"What about her?" Our gazes locked and I knew. A flutter went through my stomach. "You can't be serious."

"Think about it. We're screwed. The Novem is done for. Together they had enough combined power to hold Athena off for all these years. Divided we fall, just like Bran said. Athena is coming, Ari, and this time it's going to be different. It's going to be the end of this city."

Shivers skipped along my nerves. I rubbed my arms. "But waking a god, Sebastian? We could be releasing something even worse. And not just on us, on everyone here and maybe beyond. We have no idea what would happen."

"Let's just talk to Bran again, see what he thinks. If he agrees, then we should do it."

"Fine. We talk to him first."

EIGHTEEN

WE TOLD THE OTHERS WE'D BE BACK AND THEN HURRIED FROM the hospital. As I crossed the street, I could see the orange glow of fire in the distance. The French Quarter was burning. The fighting within the Novem must have gotten worse. Locals and tourists fled past us. I saw several kids from Presby being led by their parents. They crammed Canal Street, where EMTs, firefighters, and Bran's contingent of police tried to keep the peace, directing everyone to the hospital and to several buildings along Canal. There at least they were out of the main fighting. There were several officers trying to keep the crowd from fleeing toward the ruins of the business district—to so do meant certain death.

In the square, flames poured out of Presby's upper floors. The Novem was at war. Jackson Square had become a battlefield.

Sebastian might be right. The god might be our only hope, because once Athena launched her attack, there would be very little resistance if this kept up.

We were on the corner near the Pontalba Apartments and the Cabildo when the ground trembled beneath our feet. The stone pavers erupted, roots shooting from the ground. They wrapped around our legs, tightening until the pain made me scream.

"Get down!"

Immediately I dropped as a ball of green light came at us. Sebastian had very little time to call upon his power and cast a thick blue shield around us. The green energy hit with staggering force. The shield broke, but the power was already dispersing. *Holy shit.* Sebastian was building a ball of blue energy in his hand.

The witch lurked beneath the large oak in the corner of the park. An earth witch. A smoky green haze surrounded her. She was our age, scared shitless, and I guessed she was attacking anything that came close; I might have been too if I was trapped and confused and had no clue what was happening. Most of the families probably had no idea. They were following the lead of their family heads. They were dying for nothing, friends fighting friends. And it wasn't confined to adults. There were several fighting who were in my classes. If they knew the truth, things would be much different.

Another hit from the witch sent me to my knees, the roots still holding me tight. "Can you trap her? Get inside her head?" I yelled over the sounds of the fight, not wanting the girl to die, just to wise up and get the hell away from the square. Our eyes met and Sebastian nodded. I knew he was weakened from earlier, but he closed his eyes, drawing energy around him.

A vampire approached in a blur from behind Sebastian. I grabbed the dagger I always kept in my boot and threw it, aiming for his throat, but hitting him in the eye. The blade sank deep. It wouldn't kill him, but it would keep him down for a while. The roots finally broke. I stumbled forward as the witch broke her hold and ran away. I went for my blade and spied Bran one door down from Zoe's apartment. He and his daughter, Kieran, were covering a family as they hurried beneath the second-floor balconies, around the corner where others were there to escort them to safety.

"Is Zoe up there?" I asked, running up to him.

"They're next. We're trying to evacuate as many families as we can," he tossed over his shoulder as we followed him up the stairs.

At the landing, Bran paused to catch his breath. Blood splatters and smears covered his face, sword arm, hand, and sword. In the small space he was intimidating as hell. Kieran was a mirror image of her father, only a lot smaller and younger than me by a couple of years. It was on the tip of my tongue to ask why she hadn't gone to safety with the others, but I stayed quiet. Kieran was his only daughter, the only child he had left. I knew he'd keep her by his side. Bran had once boasted that Kieran was so talented with a sword she could've separated my head from my body when she was ten.

"We need help, Bran," I said.

My words sank in, and he knew exactly what I meant. "Oh no. No fucking way, Selkirk." He glanced from me to Sebastian and back again. "No. Not happening." He pounded on the door, calling for Zoe's parents.

"Bran." He whipped around, the point of his sword at my throat. His face was grim and completely unmovable.

"No."

Zoe opened the door. *Oh shit.* Goose bumps spread up my arms. Her eyes were milky white. The tip of Bran's sword dropped. He grabbed Zoe's shoulders. *"Zoe. Where are your mom and dad?"*

She didn't answer, not even when he shouted her name and shook her gently.

"They must be out fighting," Sebastian said.

Two vamps surged up the stairs, one hitting me in the back, sending me flying down the hall. I landed hard and rolled, ending up with the vampire on top of me. I grabbed his face, about to put all my power into it, when a sword stuck through the guy's throat, the point stopping an inch from my chin. Blood sprayed on my face. I twisted away, scrambling from underneath him as the sword withdrew and sliced the head from the body.

For a moment I couldn't move. Bran loomed in front of me, reached down, and plucked the head off the floor. Another headless body lay on the landing. Kieran, sword dripping, leaned over and picked up the head like some avenging Celtic war goddess.

"You have power, use it," Bran said roughly as I got up.

I managed to find my voice, wiping the blood from my face as best I could. "I was about to."

He walked toward Kieran, and together they tossed the heads down the stairs, a fair warning to any who might want to come up.

We herded Zoe into the apartment and shut the door. Bran went to the window to survey the scene outside. I joined him. It was getting bad. Presby was burning and across the square, one corner of an apartment block was on fire. "We have to do something," I said quietly. "What if this god is good? What if we can ask for his help in exchange for waking him?"

"You said so yourself," Sebastian added. "We're screwed."

Bran's jaw ticked as I stared at his profile. Down below, cries and breaking glass could be heard over the sounds of magic exploding and snarls and shouts. "We find out more about the god first and then decide." He glanced back at his daughter, worry on his face. "You talk to her. Bastian, Kieran, and I will keep watch. Cut all the lights. We don't want to draw attention. We do nothing"—he looked at me pointedly—"until we know more."

I drew in a deep breath and went to Zoe as Sebastian killed the lights. Kieran stepped back, a little freaked out by Zoe's white eyes. She was a fighter, not an exorcist. Neither was I, for that matter. Bran opened the door and took up position on the landing, while Kieran covered the doorway. Sebastian was the last line of defense between me and them if they failed.

The fiery light from the square lit the room in a dim, eerie glow. It made Zoe look even creepier. I knelt down in front of her.

"Zoe. It's me, Ari." I cleared my throat. "I want to talk to the god who speaks to you." Nothing. "Zoe. It's me. The god-killer."

The corners of her mouth drew back into a smile, like some puppet master was pulling the strings. "Wake me up," the strange whisper came from her lips. "Wake me up and I'll set you free."

"Who are you?" I asked. "I won't wake you up until I know who you are and why you want to return to our world."

Zoe went silent for a long moment. I was about to try to get the god talking again, but then she spoke, fast, as though uttering a prayer that hadn't been uttered since time began. "I am Yesterday. I am He who is Above. Born under the Morning

Star. I am the Sun and the Moon. Ruler of the Skies. Guardian of Pharaohs. I am the Great Falcon. I am War. I am Protection. I am He Who Comes Forth Advancing. I have opened a path. I have delivered myself from all evil things."

The room seemed to still, the sounds from outside dimming. I didn't know what had changed, but I sure as hell felt that something had. Bran stood in the doorway, his face pale, his sword arm limp, his eyes dazed.

Zoe clutched the front of my bloody shirt and pulled me so close our noses brushed. The voice was urgent and demanding. "Now bring me *back*."

Zoe shoved me away with a force that was not her own. I landed on my rear, heart pounding. The sounds from outside raged on, filling the dead silence. Explosions lit the dark room with flashes. Glass shattered down the hall, bringing everything back into focus. We were running out of time.

"What now?" I asked Bran as Zoe sat down, her legs crossed and her hands resting limply in her lap. Her eyes were locked on me. Then they shifted to Sebastian. "Wake me up and I'll set you free."

That was the offer. Made to me, and now to Sebastian. He just stood there, staring at Zoe with troubled eyes. "That's the bargain," I said. "Whoever wakes him up is set free from their curse."

"Vampirism isn't a curse. It's part of my makeup," he answered. But I could see the longing in his eyes.

"And that god can change you back. To the way you were before . . . before the temple. That's what he means." I wanted it to be true. Sebastian could go back to the way he had been. And at that moment, I knew it should be him and not me. "Right, Bran? That's what it means."

"Yeah, that's what *he* means. And if he's the father of Athena's child . . . Athena won't stand a chance."

"Who is he? Is he good? Do we wake him?"

"Yeah, he's good. But you have to remember, Athena was good once too. It's a risk. One I think we—"

Bran was hit from behind by a massive black wolf. They rolled into the apartment as Kieran shouted, leaping aside just in time. Bran and the wolf smashed through the coffee table and hit the far wall, denting the drywall. Teeth gnashed, and angry red claw marks appeared on Bran's chest. Sebastian was building energy over his hand. I ran to help Kieran as a second shifter appeared.

Through it all, Zoe sat waiting.

A vampire joined the fray on the landing. I chanced a look over my shoulder to see Sebastian shove a massive ball of energy at the wolf, knocking it off Bran. Bran recovered and swung his sword to lethal effect.

The landing was filling up. Shit. We were going to be overrun, trapped. Damn it. I exchanged a desperate glance with Sebastian. I ducked and landed a punch to the vamp's midsection, shoving my power into my fist when I did. She screamed. I spun again and grabbed her wrist, still pouring my curse into her. As she spun away from me, her arm broke off and she smashed into the wall.

Kieran killed the second shifter. But she was tiring too. Bran hurried to fight by her side.

"Ari!" I spun at Sebastian's call. Confused, I hurried over as he closed his eyes. The hairs on my arms lifted as energy, thick and suffocating, gathered in the room. His hand clamped down on my wrist. And then the scene froze.

Everything froze—but us.

"God, Sebastian. What are you doing?" My heart skipped. He was bleeding from the nose. I reached out but he caught my hand.

"Go to Zoe. Wake up the god."

"But—"

"Hurry. I can't hold them all for long. This is what we've been after. A way to end your curse. A way to end Athena."

I should've been jumping at the chance. And yet, it didn't feel right. I couldn't believe I was saying this, but, "I'm a god-killer, Sebastian. If this god rises and wreaks havoc, I'll need to stop him. I can't do that if I don't have my power. I can't risk giving it up until all this"—I waved my hand—"chaos with Athena is over. My chance lies with the Hands. This is *your* chance. You take it." Pain squeezed my chest. "You do it. You never wanted to be a vampire. You never would have been if it wasn't for me."

He shook his head, frowning. "No—"

I grabbed his shoulders. "Yes. You have to. It's killing you, being what you are now. I can see it." My throat went thick. "It's your turn. Mine will come later. If we raise this god, I'm the insurance policy. If all goes to shit and he's crazy like Athena, I'm the only one who can kill him. And if he fails, I'll still need my power to bargain with Athena. She'll kill me if I'm curse free. It means her child will never be resurrected."

Sebastian trembled from the massive amount of power he was using to freeze our tiny corner of the world. He couldn't keep it up much longer. His gaze flicked to the frozen battle on the landing. Relief filled me. He was going to do it. He gave me a sharp nod, swiped at the blood trickling from his nose, and then stepped back.

"If this works, I'll meet you someplace safe . . . at the hospital," he said. "Just stay out of trouble until then." With a parting look, he closed his eyes and raised his hands, pulling in energy and moving in a beautiful flowing motion, gathering it like I'd once seen him do in his father's garden. And then he shot out his arms, opening his eyes. They flashed bright blue. I was pushed by the force, stumbling as I watched our attackers disintegrate.

In the blink of an eye, Sebastian had Zoe in his arms and was gone.

Gone.

And we were left stunned by the magnitude of his power.

Bran recovered and stalked toward me. "What has he done?"

"He's going to wake the god."

"Goddamn it, Selkirk! We agreed!"

"But you said—"

"I never got to finish what I was saying. Do you know what he's waking? A supreme fucking deity!"

"Who—"

He seized Kieran's and my wrists. "We're getting out of this apartment. If I'm going to fight, I'll do it out in the open."

"Bran." I pulled against him. "Wait. Who is the god?"

I was almost afraid to know.

NINETEEN

His power gave out a few feet above his grandmother's garden. Not the location he'd been aiming for, but at least it wasn't pavement. They landed with a thud, his back hitting the ground first, then Zoe's weight hitting him from the front, knocking the breath from his lungs. He released her, and she rolled off him. His muscles trembled, his mind was exhausted, and pain shot arcs through his brain. Nausea rolled through his gut. Too much power; he'd used too much. It took several seconds for his vision to focus, the blurry night stars finally snapping back into place.

Hell, he hadn't even realized he could draw that much power.

Zoe sat up and looked around with her possessed eyes as he slowly pushed himself to a sitting position. She waited until he drew in several ragged breaths and said, "Now wake me up."

Sebastian's entire body was shaking hard now. Keeping his balance, even in a sitting position, was difficult. "Just . . . give me a minute."

She grabbed his arm and leaned in close. "I have waited long. Too long."

"Then you won't mind a couple more minutes. I don't even know how to wake you up."

"You come to me, to my world, and speak my names to my body. Then I will live again in the mortal realm."

"And then what? You tear into my world and destroy everything?"

"Not everything. You fear for your world, your city, your family. Have no fear, young Mistborn. I have no desire to destroy that which is beyond my goal."

Yeah. If only he could believe that. Still, the alternative—the city was already being destroyed. People he knew were hurt or dying. Already dead.

Zoe leaned forward and took Sebastian's hands. Hers were small, so thin and delicate that he could crush them. Zoe closed her eyes and spoke words he could not understand but knew were of an ancient, maybe even lost language. Power gathered around them, the rush of it surrounding them and energizing him. The lights from the garden lanterns dimmed, then went out.

"What are you doing?"

"Hush," she whispered.

Blackness enveloped them. And then weightlessness.

One second Sebastian was sitting in the soft grass and the next he was standing alone somewhere else entirely. His knees buckled, but he managed to catch himself, gasping and disoriented.

Warmth seeped into his body. It was a rejuvenating sensation that made him stand a little straighter and think a little more clearly. He blinked a few times and pulled fresh nighttime air into his lungs. He wasn't exactly sure what had happened, but he knew he was no longer in the garden. This wasn't the French Quarter. Hell, this wasn't even his world.

Colossal columns were set in a rectangular pattern around a stone floor, with no walls or roof. The columns were as thick and tall as old California redwoods, their bases alone a story high. Every inch was carved and painted in bright colors.

A temple. He was in a temple. One made for giants.

On three sides, the land dropped sharply into black water. Twinkling stars reflected on the surface. There were other islands out there in the darkness, and he could see temples and palaces with fires burning in large basins and torches. Lush gardens fell over balconies, and old reed boats floated in the water with lanterns hung from their high curved ends.

On the fourth side of the temple, the land dipped, leading down into a courtyard filled with tall palms, flowering trees, and plants with blossoms as big as dinner plates. A pool. And beyond that was a long gallery of columns that led into an enormous temple that dwarfed the one where he stood.

The enormity of the place and situation hit him. "Where am I?" he whispered to himself.

"Sekhet Hetepet. *Land of my father. Part of the Egyptian Otherworld."*

Sebastian spun toward the deep voice, ready to defend himself, but his hands fell limp at his side as he got his first look at the god. Bran's words echoed in his head. Old. Primal. Deity. *The god watched him. Even without speech, without movement, he seemed to bleed power through his pores. The god had wings like a falcon and the body of a man. He wore some sort of linen skirt and nothing else except a large collar made up of beads, gems, and gold. His skin was a smooth charcoal black, and the tattoos that covered his body were done in faded blues and reds and greens. Bluish green lined his eyes, and his strange irises glowed bright within the darkness of his face. One eye like the sun, one eye like the moon. They were mesmerizing. Haunting. And they drew him in like a moth to a flame. He wanted to stare into those eyes forever.*

Sebastian did a mental head shake. His reaction wasn't physical attraction. There was no tug in his belly like he had with Ari. But this god . . . being near him was like being drawn to an exotic predator, one that lured you in despite the risks.

Wait. One eye like the moon. One like the sun.

Shock burst in his gut. Oh shit. He knew who this was. Horus. Supreme Egyptian deity. Son of Osiris and Isis.

"You know who I am."

Sebastian nodded. His mouth had gone dry.

"I am not real, Sebastian Lamarliere. My body still sleeps. This is my spirit form. In your world I have many forms. You must call my true form back from Sleep. You must breathe life into my true names. Names have great power."

The soft pad of steps somewhere behind him made him turn. A shadow emerged from between the massive columns. Sebastian's jaw went slack at the sight of the huge black lioness. Her gigantic paws slapped the stone as she paced slowly back and forth.

She was tense and impatient and looked hungry as hell. She shifted suddenly into a sleek Egyptian cat, walked into a dark shadow, then reappeared as a lioness again.

"She shifts when she is agitated," Horus said. "No harm will come to you here, Mistborn. Wake me up and I'll set you free."

"You can't free me," he said, finding his voice and facing the god again. "I'm a vampire. I've taken blood. My body has already made the change."

Horus raised an eyebrow. "Reversing the effects of blood on the body is as simple as healing. Doubting me . . . I am not used to such things."

"You might not be used to a lot of things," Sebastian said carefully. "People don't really believe in the old gods anymore. The world is not as you might remember it. You might not like what you find."

"I know what I will find. I have only been asleep for a short time."

Sebastian was pretty sure his idea of a short time and the god's were totally different. "Can you kill Athena?"

"She is a worthy adversary, with many of her father's talents and powers." The god shrugged. "We shall see."

Horus stared out over the dark, glittering landscape of the Egyptian Otherworld. The only sound was the water lapping at the cliffs and the lioness pacing behind them, randomly shifting from huge predator to small feline, her footfalls telling him when she was lion and when she was not.

Sebastian tipped his head back, amazed at how clear and how impossibly bright the stars were in this place. As he looked, a subtle shift happened, and the sky took on the appearance of a roof, a dome over the landscape made of inky blue tiles painted with yellow and white stars. So close. He lifted his hand.

"Reach. Jump. Fly for days, months, years," Horus said. "And you will never reach them. It is the Sleeping Sky. Painted by the first gods, then given life and infinite space. This is the sky in which gods go to sleep. They are the brightest stars. . . ."

Sebastian stared hard at the glittering stars. They glowed and winked and burned like diamonds held up to a flame. In one moment, they seemed as far away as the stars in his own sky and in another, close enough for him to touch.

But he hadn't come here to sightsee. He'd come for help. And that meant making sure Horus knew exactly what was required of him if Sebastian was going to wake the god from his sleep.

Sebastian began his long-winded terms of the bargain he was about to make, knowing he treaded on thin ice. He felt like he'd spoken for hours, covering every possible angle.

Horus, surprisingly, agreed to everything, which made Sebastian relieved and suspicious. But there was no turning back now as the god began the ritual necessary for Sebastian to speak his names. Sebastian followed him through the lofty columns to the center of the temple. There was a table there, one he hadn't remembered seeing before. On it was a tall golden idol of a male with the head of a falcon, the body of a man, and a large sun disk on his head. In his hand was a staff with a painted eye. Beneath the lower rim of the eye, a line curved down and around like a tail. Next to this line, another shorter line had been drawn straight down and closer to the inside corner of the eye.

He'd seen this eye many times before in books and on statues. The Eye of Horus.

On the table were three bowls: one of black liquid, one of red, and one of bluish green. Horus picked up a small dagger from the table.

He offered Sebastian the blade. "You must squeeze a drop of your blood into each bowl."

Sebastian slit his finger, then squeezed three drops into the bowls.

Horus dipped his finger into one of the bowls. "Close your mouth and face me," he said.

Fear spiked through him at the god's words. He had to concentrate on keeping his feet planted. But he'd come this far. He thought of what was happening in his world, the fighting, the chaos, the fires. . . .

Horus's strange eyes grew brighter as he lifted his finger and touched Sebastian's mouth. The contact sent the creepiest buzz through him as Horus traced the blue paint over the outer edge of Sebastian's top and bottom lip, making the shape of what felt like an eye. Horus took another finger and dipped it in black, making a small line down his chin, and then, with the red, he made a second line. Just like the eye on the staff.

"You speak now through the Eye."

When Horus instructed him to draw the eye over the god's mouth, Sebastian went cold. He wanted to bolt, to get the hell out of there, but he didn't move. As much as he didn't want to touch Horus, he dipped his finger in the blue and, with a shaky hand, drew the eye around Horus's lips, followed by two lines down his chin in the red and black.

Sweat rolled down his back. The eye around Horus's mouth looked eerie and grim, almost violent in a way. Like war paint, something with meaning and power.

"I too speak through the Eye, and thus my words are binding." Horus then repeated everything Sebastian had requested in exchange for the awakening, word for word. "Should I break this vow, my spirit will be pulled by the Eye, through my mouth, releasing me from my body once again. Now you must wake me or suffer the same."

Sebastian's heart was pounding so hard he thought he saw stars of a different kind. He gulped. The paint on his lips felt strange as he gave a sharp nod, wondering if this was the smartest thing he'd ever done—or the very worst.

Horus began to say strange and ancient-sounding names. Sebastian repeated them slowly. One after another. The air warbled. As he said the names, he felt the paint sinking into his skin and tingling around his mouth, then down his throat, and into his chest as though it had settled into his lungs. Sebastian felt as though he was breathing life into the names as they came out of his mouth.

Then, carefully, he reached up and felt his mouth. It was dry. There was no paint. It had disappeared.

Beyond Horus's shoulder, one of the stars in the painted sky grew brighter. Slowly its light was pulled downward in a long stream, growing more brilliant as it touched Horus. The more names that were spoken, the brighter the light that filled him.

As the last name was spoken, Sebastian shielded his eyes. The light surrounded Horus, illuminating his form. Then, in a flash, the star was gone, and before Sebastian stood the tanned figure of a man with a shaved head, dressed in linen. Horus was just as impressive and intimidating now as he had been in his spirit form.

"Now let's go get my child."

TWENTY

"Bran!" I yelled after him as we hurried down the stairs. "Damn it, what god is it?"

An explosion hit the apartment. Pieces of plaster fell from the ceiling as the building shook. We made it outside just as the stairwell collapsed in a heap of drywall, wood, and plaster.

Coughing, I ran down the street. All around me, the war raged on. Where people weren't fighting, they were pulling the wounded to safety or evacuating families from the apartments. On the corner of St. Peter and Chartres, Bran slid to a sudden stop. Slamming into him was like slamming into a brick wall. With one final cough and spit, I stepped around him to see what had stopped him cold.

Athena's army. Minions and creatures of lore spilled into

the square from the side streets. Harpies, Minotaur, one-eyed cyclops, sirens, vampires, a few arachnid/human hybrids . . .

My heart sank. It was over.

Kieran came to stand at my other shoulder. And I could tell from their silence, they felt what I did: defeat. Yeah, we'd fight to the bitter end, but inside we knew there was no way to beat them all. There were just too many against an already wounded, divided, exhausted foe. The Novem and New 2 as we knew them would end tonight unless Sebastian came through. Unless, by some miracle, I found the Hands and stopped Athena before things got worse.

A child screamed. Turning, I saw my father carrying a little boy and holding the hand of his young mother. We still had time to get the remaining families out of the square. "Most of the apartments are cleared," my father said as he hurried past us. "Don't engage unless you have to. Help whoever you can to safety."

A small family of four clung to the shadows of a storefront, afraid to move. I went to help them, but the River Witch appeared and helped them cross. *What the hell is he doing here?* Once the family was on their way down Chartres, away from the square, I grabbed his arm. "What are you doing here? Where are the kids?"

He spun around, the hood of his cloak slipping. "Still at the hospital." His withered old face held no emotion as he stared at me and then said, "You're all going to die, and you're too stupid to save them."

I blinked at him, shocked by the venom in his tone.

"Use your power, gorgon. What are you waiting for?" He shoved me in the belly with the end of his cane. I reacted without thinking, grabbing it and jerking it past my side, pulling him closer to me in the process. I had him by the throat.

He tried to laugh, but could only wheeze. "So rudimentary. Only by touch. You're not a true god-killer until you can do it with your *eyes*. There's a reason they look the way they do, clear and reflective. . . ." The witch lifted his cane and power erupted from it, hitting a line of minions running at us. They burst into a shower of ashes. A powerful staff, not a simple cane.

I stared hard at him, my grip softening. I'd always thought I had to touch in order for my power to work. Could he be right? Could I do it now?

"Ari!" My father's shout jerked me back into the here and now. He was fighting his way to me, swarmed by minions. I started for him. He swung to behead one minion, but a harpy flew in and plucked his sword from his hand. His bloodied hands couldn't hold on, and it slipped from his grasp. I shoved away from the witch. My father leaped, grabbing the harpy's ankle, kicking the minion coming at him and then grappling with the harpy. Its leathery wings beat frantically, unable to gain upward momentum.

A sword buried itself in the harpy's chest, the creature's shriek so high-pitched and loud, I had to cover my ears. It was Bran's sword sticking out of its chest; I'd recognize it anywhere. I tracked back and found him across the street. My father and the harpy dropped as Bran began hand-to-hand combat, shouting at Kieran nearby. He urged her to run, to get the hell out of the melee.

I grabbed my father's blade from the ground and clotheslined a minion running toward me, then dropped to my knee and stabbed it in the heart. After that came another. And another. With every kill I made, with every use of the blade and my power, my hopes sank. We were getting nowhere. And I was getting no closer to my father's side. The witch's words echoed in my head as I fought, and I tried like hell to connect my power to my gaze. It was a move I had never practiced, and my attempts were pathetic. There just wasn't time to concentrate. Opponents were coming at me with blistering speed, keeping me too occupied with staying alive.

As I destroyed another minion, a bright flash appeared in the wide mall in front of the cathedral. In its wake stood Athena, Artemis, and Apollo in their shining armor. Grim faces assessed the battle. Athena's statuesque form surveyed the scene with a critical eye. The sides of her raven hair were braided in two small war braids, beaded with bone, and pulled back behind her head.

She smiled at Presby burning and gestured for the others to follow her inside the building. Menai and Melinoe were there too, and they took up positions to guard the entrance, as Athena and her brother and sister disappeared inside.

I darted through the violence, dispatching any comers as I went. In the park, I edged close to one of the dark corners. Suddenly the windows in Presby blew out, sending a shower of glass onto those below. The force was so great, glass pinged the iron fence bars in front of me. A few shards sliced my forearm and shoulder, my scalp, too, as I ducked and dove behind a nearby tree.

Looked like Athena had discovered that Anesidora's Jar was gone.

Seconds later the goddess stormed from the building, saying something to Menai. Menai notched two arrows and aimed into the melee. I looked for her target, wondering how she could make out anything in the chaos. She must have found it because she stilled, her gaze sharpening.

I followed her line of sight to where it rested on my father fighting Athena's minions like a hero of old. *No.* Dread washed over me, cold and swift. Heart in my throat, I ran. "No!" But the arrows were let loose.

I shouldered my way to him, turning anything I touched into stone. But it wasn't enough. I couldn't outrun those arrows. They flew with divine precision through the melee and hit my father, one in each shoulder. The force sent him flying into the air, the arrows pinning him to a restaurant's door.

I yelled his name, trying like mad to get to him. Somehow he heard me and went still. "Stay back!" He struggled, cursing and kicking at two minions who tried to approach him. Then he was swamped.

Oh God. No.

"Dad!"

I stabbed a minion who challenged me, sweeping him off his feet with a low roundhouse and then stabbing with all the anger and horror I felt. I'd cut through every damn one of them if I had to. Tears stung my eyes, desperation making me crazed. I darted forward only to be pulled back. I swung around with a frustrated growl, slicing with my blade. A hand grabbed my wrist. Kieran. Dear God. I'd almost stabbed her.

Heart pounding, I stayed there locked with her for a moment before stepping back. The arrows were torn from my father's shoulders, then he was being led to the cathedral where Athena waited. Kieran and I moved into the shadows, in the corner by the fence, its trees and bushes giving us enough darkness to hide.

Athena's voice carried, projecting over the square, as she grabbed my father's chin. "Where is the jar?" she demanded.

"The jar doesn't matter. The Hands aren't inside."

"Where are they?"

"The only one who knows that is dead," my father answered.

Their voices dropped, and I could only pick up bits and pieces. They spoke about Josephine, her death. Sebastian's name was mentioned. Athena thought that as her grandson, he might know the location of the Hands. Athena drew Melinoe aside, and I had to wonder if she was giving orders to the ghostly goddess to seek out Josephine's soul, if she had one. Mel gave a sharp nod and took off, disappearing into thin air.

My father was taken into the cathedral, followed by the gods. Athena stopped on the steps, looking out over the square. Her head turned our way, and I got the feeling she knew exactly where I was.

"What now?" Kieran asked as Athena went into the cathedral.

"I need to get the Hands. Without them, I have nothing to bargain with when I get inside that church and, hopefully, get my father *out*."

"I'm coming with you," she announced with a stubborn expression that reminded me of Bran. "I'm not running away with the rest of the children." That thought obviously appalled her.

"He just wants you to be safe."

"I'm safer with a sword in my hand and a foe to fight. I've been training since I could walk. My great-grandfather is a war god; I'm not running away like some coward. I'm coming with you. If you tell me no, I'll follow you anyway."

She was arrogant and demanding like her father too. "Suit yourself."

Kieran and I snuck away from the square toward the river. Once we made it to the Riverwalk, we hightailed it along the waterfront, then to Canal, and finally to Charity Hospital. Josephine was dead, the Hands . . . who knew. My only options were to wait for Sebastian or to go back to Arnaud House for the journals I'd dropped in hopes I'd find a clue about the Hands within the pages.

The hospital was packed with the injured and the scared. We muscled our way inside, getting some strange looks because of our bloodied state. The waiting room was filled, but the kids were nowhere to be seen. I went to the front desk but found a nurse on my way, stopping her to ask about Crank. Then we were taking the stairs to the third floor to find her room.

The room was peaceful and quiet, such a sharp contrast to the chaos of where we'd just been and the things we had done to survive. Stepping into the room was like stepping onto another planet.

Crank looked so small in the bed. Her eyes were closed. The monitors beeped steadily. I picked up her chart, noticing the blood on my hands, the way it had filled in the creases and wrinkles and lines in my palm, and crept under my fingernails. . . .

"Ari," Kieran whispered.

I jumped. Crank's eyes were open. "Hey," I said, immediately going to her side.

"Jeez. You look like shit," she murmured in a sleepy voice. "Who's that?"

"Bran's daughter, Kieran. Has the doctor been in yet?"

She nodded and swallowed, the action taking some effort. "All's well. Going to be A-OK." She gave a limp thumbs-up. "The guys were here. They left a little while ago with the lady."

"What lady?"

"The witch," Crank answered, closing her eyes. "So pretty."

"Where did they go? Did they say?"

She didn't know. *Damn it.*

"So the witch is bad?" Kieran asked, confused.

"I don't know. I think it might be the drugs talking. The only witch that was here before was the River Witch, and *he* is definitely not pretty. He also said he left the kids here at the hospital."

"All right," Kieran said, obviously having no clue who I was talking about. "Now what?"

"Well, we can wait for Sebastian to show up or head back into the Quarter for Josephine's journals. It's a shot in the dark, but it's the only thing I know of that might give us a clue on the Hands."

"How about I round up some water or something? Then we

can leave Sebastian a note, tell him where we went and to wait for us to get back."

I slumped on the chair. "Okay."

Kieran washed her hands and face in the sink in the small bathroom before leaving. When she was gone, I did the same, watching the blood swirl down the drain. It was even in my hair, staining the white red and black. Tiny spray patterns of blood stuck to my neck, my face, ears, and hands. I scrubbed my face, hands, forearms, and neck, before retying my hair and studying my reflection in the mirror. I looked bruised and drawn. After all I'd seen and done, I understood the solemn expression in my eyes. It was in my father's eyes at times. In Bran's. In Sebastian's and Michel's. "Haunted" might be the right word.

You're not a true god-killer until you can do it with your eyes. There's a reason they look the way they do, clear and reflective.

The witch's words taunted me. I rinsed my mouth, spitting out blood from a cut inside my lip, and then blew my nose, trying to get out the fine mist of blood I'd inhaled during the battle. Tears stung my eyes. I pressed my cold hands against my eyelids and drew in a deep breath, letting it out slowly. Then I left the bathroom and sat down.

Kieran came back a few minutes later. She handed me a bag of chips and a bottled water. I devoured the chips and drank half the bottle. "I don't suppose you speak French, do you?"

She shook her head. "Just Gaelic and English, why?"

"The journals are probably written in French."

"There are tons of people around here who can read French. We'll bring them back here, find someone to help us, and maybe by that time Sebastian will be back with reinforcements."

If I didn't move now, there was a good possibility exhaustion would win. I stood up, my muscles already stiff, downed the last of the water, and wrote a quick note to Sebastian.

Twenty-One

Kieran and I jogged across Canal and cut down Royal Street. The power was out, and it was eerily quiet for a block or two. Then came the screams, the gunfire, and the magic. Packs of Athena's creatures had broken off from the main battle to ravage homes and shops. We'd slowed to a fast walk, sticking to the shadows, passing harpies rifling through shops, throwing stuff into the street, eating what they found in the restaurants, and fighting over items they wanted. A few of those people holed up in their homes were making their stands and keeping the minions at bay.

A few times we were forced to duck into empty stores or alleys as Athena's creatures passed by. In one alley, we tripped over the bodies of three disemboweled musicians. It was dark, but not dark enough to hide the horror done to them. My stomach turned, and I tried to control my breathing so as not to be sick.

"My father says part of war is waged inside your own mind," Kieran said in a near whisper as we crept down the street. "Being able to distance yourself from what lies on the ground"—she stepped over the body of a shifter—"to build a barrier between your emotions and the sights, sounds, smells of death, and let it go. Let them go," she added quietly.

Seeing the carnage—the dead, the dying, those caught in the middle—I knew her father was right. During the fighting, it was easy to focus, to exist in your own little pocket where all that mattered was strike and counterstrike, and being aware of what was happening directly around you. But as soon as you stopped and looked around—even for just a moment—you made yourself vulnerable to the horrors. You made yourself distracted. So you learned how to distance your mind, to prevent yourself from fully processing the devastation, knowing you wouldn't be able to handle it if you did.

After what seemed like forever, we made it to Josephine's house. The mansion rose from the dark corner like a gray specter. The victims of our earlier fight still lay in the street, including the ghostly white pieces of the bear and what had once been Gabriel Baptiste.

Knowing the innocent victims of a mass murderer lurked inside made the house even more sinister than it appeared. At the south end of the house was the tunnel that led into the courtyard. One black sconce on the brick was broken, the other lit, a small gas flame flickering. The light should've been welcoming, but it only added another layer of eeriness to the scene.

"The journals should be just inside the front door, in the entry hall," I whispered. "Ready?"

Kieran reached over her shoulder and slid her sword from its sheath. "Ready."

We stepped away from the shadows.

"Shit," Kieran whispered, her hand grabbing my shoulder. "There."

We paused in the middle of the street. Shadows loomed in the courtyard tunnel. Two tall figures moved with confident strides, growing larger and larger as they approached. We backed up slowly as they passed through the dim light at the head of the tunnel.

Electric goose bumps stung my skin. I sucked in a breath. Sebastian was back.

The god who strode next to him with a cat trotting by his side made my insides shrink. Every muscle in my body went tight as some primal instinct said: *Run.*

"Holy cow," Kieran breathed.

The god's skin was smooth and bronze. Head shaved. He wore a loose linen shirt, the sleeves rolled to his elbows, and linen pants of the same natural color. His toes peeked out from sandals. He was tall and his arms were strong, devoid of hair and inked with faded blue tattoos. I felt his power from where I stood, and it made my heart pound.

I couldn't look away, too mesmerized by the predator. Kieran was frozen beside me. Holy hell. The eyes . . . *Look at the eyes.* And then it hit me like a thunderbolt. My knees went weak.

The god moved closer, a knowing quirk to his lips. "I take it no introductions are necessary."

My heart leaped wildly. Even his voice rang deep with power. I shook my head. I'd studied the gods in school. I knew. I had no idea how I remained standing—standing there . . . with a supreme deity.

Bran was right, we were screwed.

Horus. God of the Sky. Son of Isis and Osiris. Falcon. Said to have one eye like the sun and one like the moon. I'd read that strange description in school, and those words, that image, had stayed locked in my mind. And now I was facing the real deal. One sun-colored iris and one as pale as a high full moon glowed faintly from kohl-rimmed eyes. Up close, I saw that the faded tattoos on his arms were all hieroglyphics.

My face must have shown my shock, my fear, my disbelief,

because Horus said in a voice brimming with ancient knowledge, "I mean you no harm. I cannot harm you, even if I wanted to." He cast a glance at Sebastian, and I got his meaning. Sebastian had made his terms, and obviously the god had accepted.

Thank God for small miracles.

The cat weaved its sleek body between Horus's legs. The light from the gas lantern bounced off its glossy coat, and I saw that it wasn't entirely black like I'd thought. The tips of its hairs were black, but the color faded to a light brown at its roots. It had long legs and a wedged-shaped face. Its ears were larger than the average cat's, and it stared at me with strange yellow eyes. It looked foreign and feral, yet sophisticated and graceful. The cat nudged Horus's leg. He reached down and it leaped into his arms, then climbed onto the god's shoulder, where it draped itself, its tail curling around his neck.

"Are you okay?" I asked, turning my attention to Sebastian. He appeared fine, less weary than before. His expression was solemn, though; his eyes gave nothing away.

"Fine. What are you doing here?"

"I came back to get the journals. We're trying to find the Hands. My father has been captured by Athena. She's—" The cat hissed and Horus's eyes grew brighter, the power emanating from him pulsing out in an oppressing wave. It was brief, but holy hell was it strong.

The god lifted his head and looked around, his movements reminding me of a bird of prey. The falcon. "She's here."

"Yes. At the cathedral. She'll tear the city apart trying to find the Hands."

"And Crank," Sebastian asked, worry making his eyebrows draw together in a frown. "Have you heard anything? And the kids?"

"The kids . . . I don't know. They're not at the hospital. Crank is in her room, loopy right now, but she's going to be all right."

Horus spun on his heel and strode down the street.

Shit. "Wait!" Spurred, I ran after him. "What are you going to do?"

He stopped. "Stop Athena and reunite with my child. Do you object?"

"No. No, of course not." I just hadn't thought it would be so . . . simple.

Horus regarded me for a second, then dipped his head curtly and strode off with his cat. As I watched him, I wondered if this was truly the end.

Kieran and Sebastian came up to stand beside me. For a moment we just stayed there and watched. As the god passed through a swath of light, his cat transformed into a black lioness.

Then they were swallowed up by darkness.

Heart racing, I glanced at Sebastian's profile, wondering if he was changed. Had Horus already lifted his "curse"? He looked the same, had the same vivid coloring, the same magnetic pull. "He hasn't changed you back," I said.

"No, not yet."

"What happened to Zoe?"

"Horus sent her back to her family."

"Did he say anything about Athena, or the child?"

"Not really."

"Okay . . . Well, we should stick to our plan," I said, conviction settling over me. "Horus isn't just going up against Athena. Artemis and Apollo are there too. If something goes wrong, we still need the Hands. I'm not losing my father or this city. The journals should be just inside the door. I'll get them."

"You don't need to. I know where Josephine hid the Hands."

I stopped, stunned. Sounds echoed nearby. Quickly we moved into the tunnel of the courtyard, snuffing out the gas flame.

"The last things she said to me," Sebastian said, "were all about attending mass, making sure I kept with tradition and sat in the front pew. She never cared before whether I went to mass or not. It was her thing, not mine. It was a message. 'Sit in the front row, like all the Arnauds, in front of the floor crypt of Andres Almonester y Roxas.'"

"I know that grave," I said. "It's marked by a flat stone in the floor of the church."

"I know it too," Kieran added. "Only problem is Athena's there, in the cathedral."

And that was the rub. We could waltz right in, go through the blood-bound vows she'd offered to make me, and then hope the Hands were really there in the cathedral. If they were, I wouldn't be able to turn back. I'd have to resurrect her child. And she would have to leave the city.

Unless Athena was dead by the time I got there.

"Come on," I said. "Either way, we're going to the cathedral." We began the short hike toward the square, keeping to the shadows and ducking out of trouble when we needed to.

TWENTY-TWO

THE FIRE THAT HAD ENGULFED PRESBY WAS OUT, BUT FLAMES raged through the Pontalba Apartments along St. Ann. The inferno lit up the square and the battle. It looked as though some of the Novem had pulled together, presenting a united front against Athena's minions. We paused at the corner of the Cabildo, gazing through the wrought-iron gate that ran from arch to arch along the building's ground-floor gallery. Spikes topped those fences and had been put to gory use by minion and Novem alike.

"We're going to have to run for it," Sebastian said. "Ready?"

We ended up fighting our way toward the steps of the cathedral. Bran was on the corner of St. Ann, cutting through minions. Kieran let out a sound of alarm, wanting desperately to leap to his defense. But she stayed by my side, knowing he didn't want her in the fight—and knowing her presence might distract him. Michel was in front of Presby, battling three hideous crones. Sebastian started for his father, then stopped. "Go," I said. "We'll be fine. I'm the safest one here." And that was the truth. I was Athena's hope, after all. Every minion I'd taken down, every creature that had come at me had orders not to kill—I was sure about that.

"No, I'm not leaving you. Just hold on one second," he said, gathering power to him, building it and building it, then letting it fly at the crones. They were struck hard, the force lifting them off their feet and sending them smashing through Presby's broken ground-floor windows. Michel swung around, his gaze finding Sebastian's. With a curt nod, he was off to help Bran.

As we hurried to the cathedral steps, a dark-haired figure sauntered out and stopped with a carnal smile on her face. Her gaze skipped over me with a slight roll of insignificance and then zeroed in on Sebastian. "Bastian. Finally we have a chance to . . . reconnect. I so enjoyed our time together the other night. I've missed you."

Hate burned through my chest. My power uncoiled, making my pulse leap. Zaria was a user and a liar and a malicious soul. Sebastian's hand on my arm distracted the serpent inside me. It calmed, grudgingly. He glared at her, his profile cold and dark.

The spark in the air, the heavy weight of energy, was coming from him.

"Oh, come now." Zaria pouted. "I'd hate to have to kill you."

He looked at me. "This won't take long. I'll see you inside."

I continued to stare daggers at her. "Make her pay, Sebastian," I said in a tight voice. "And make it last."

Zaria snorted and braced for attack. They advanced. Kieran and I ducked as they slammed into each other, grappling and shooting straight into the air. It was hard to pull myself away, but this was his battle and his right to deal justice to one who unequivocally deserved it.

Three harpies swooped down from the church's steeples to land in front of me. They were over six feet tall, with black eyes ringed in yellow, leathery skin, and wings tipped with razor-sharp claws.

"Move," I told them.

"You may pass," one of them hissed in a high-pitched voice. She peered at Kieran. "You, little girl, may not."

Still hyped up from the fight moments ago, Kieran lifted her sword. "And how would you like my sword shoved up your—"

"Let her pass," I cut in before things got serious, "or we can add three more statues to the square. Your choice."

The harpies screeched at us, but they moved aside with threats to peck out our eyes, nibble on our entrails, and make coats out of our sweet young skins.

I walked into the vestibule. The gift shop to my left had been ransacked. The votive stand with its burning candles had been upended. The prayer room to the right was occupied by a huge, troll-like creature, sitting on the floor with its legs stuck through the busted-out entryway. It was crunching on something bloody. Kieran made a soft grunt of horror. My gag reflex kicked in. Quickly I put my hand on one of the nave doors and pushed.

Now or never. And I sure as hell hoped I had the power to resurrect Athena's child, because if I didn't . . .

The long, checkered aisle, flanked by columns and flags, and the balcony of the second-story gallery spread out before us, leading my gaze straight to the nave's sanctuary and altar table. Athena sat on the table, swinging her feet, watching me as we approached. High behind her and the table, my father was bound to the massive sanctuary statue, each wrist tied to the columns that framed the statue. His feet were together and shot through with an arrow that pinned them to the stone beneath. Athena's version of a crucifixion.

I gritted my teeth, forcing calm into the anger I had at seeing him like that. My dad's head lifted, and he paled. If he had his way, I'd be fleeing past The Rim by now. But that wasn't me. I'd always come for him. *Always.* Whether he liked it or not. He'd do the same for me.

Artemis and Apollo stood at the end of the aisle, one on either side, intimidating as hell in their battle regalia. There was no sign of Horus anywhere, and I had a feeling something had gone wrong, terribly wrong.

Athena gripped the edges of the altar table where she sat, her attention glued on me. There was no expression on her face, which surprised me because I expected her to be smiling in that arrogant, knowing way of hers. But there was nothing but intensity. She must believe she was close to being reunited with her child.

I passed Artemis and Apollo, Kieran sticking to my side. I'd been told that after the war between the gods, after Athena had gone nuts and killed her father and his supporters, the surviving gods had fallen into line, Athena too powerful with Zeus's lightning bolt and his Aegis, a powerful breastplate and shield that made its wearer virtually indestructible. Eventually she'd lost the Aegis. And yet her brother and sister remained by her side. I knew from Menai that Athena had some hold over Artemis, but as for Apollo, I had no idea why he stayed with Athena.

Athena wore her awful bodysuit, made from the dark-olive skin of the Titan monster Typhon, sewn together, hugging her body from neck to wrist to ankle, sometimes shifting and moving, like a living thing on her body. Novem legend differed from what the rest of the world knew; the Aegis Athena had lost was actually made from the skin of the king of the Titans, Zeus's own father, Cronos. When Zeus, and then Athena, wore it in battle, it made them invincible.

"You have the Hands, gorgon?" Athena asked in a neutral tone.

"I know where they are, yes."

Her earthy green eyes flared with desperation and hope. She hopped off the altar and strode across the crimson carpet. At nearly six feet tall and standing two steps higher, she towered over me. "You will revive my child?"

I swallowed. Inside I was shaking, and it took some effort to keep the trembling from my voice. "If you agree to leave me and my friends, my family and theirs, my descendants and theirs, the city and *everyone* in it alone, unharmed—by your hand, your command, or your influence—forever."

"That is a tall request for one so . . . small."

"A small concession compared to holding your child again. After I do this, you must also agree to remove my curse."

Her full lips dipped into a frown. "Anything else?"

"No, that about does it," I answered, noticing that she seemed a little pale, her breathing subtly shallow. She hadn't fully healed from our last meeting.

"The Hands," she prompted.

I drew in a deep breath and glanced at Kieran. Together we went to the right side of the church and found the long marble slab etched with the name ANDRES ALMONESTER Y ROXAS.

Athena knelt down. "Here?" she asked, her voice tight. "Beneath this stone?"

"Yes. That's where Josephine hid them."

Please be right, Sebastian. Please be right.

She waved us away, her focus on the stone as she ran her hands over the surface. A faint green light appeared beneath her hand and traveled around the seam of the slab. As she lifted her hand, the stone rose. The sound grated through the cathedral. A thud shook the floor as she set the heavy stone aside.

I held my breath as she peered inside, using her power to raise the Hands from their hiding place. My breath caught in relief and wonder. They were just as I remembered. A stone basket cradled by two strong hands, broken off at the wrists. Athena grabbed the statue with care. As I stared at her profile, I could only imagine what must be running through her head and her heart.

Finally she rose with her treasure. Her throat worked, and I caught the briefest flash of emotion in her glistening eyes. Anguish. Pain. Fear of feeling happiness just yet. As she carried the basket to the altar table and placed it on top, I noticed Artemis had tears in her eyes.

Now it was all up to me.

But first we had to make our bargain binding. The doors to the cathedral slammed shut with a heart-stopping bang, Athena using her power to cut off my main escape route. When the sound faded away, she said in a low, emotionless tone, "Step up to my altar." A shiver crawled up my spine.

Squaring my shoulders, I left Kieran with what I hoped was a reassuring nod, stepped onto the raised sanctuary, and walked to the altar.

At the table, I looked at the child inside the basket, eyes open, its body covered in a blanket, one chubby hand clutching the end. A bowl divided into two separate sides appeared on the altar, along with a thin, wicked-looking blade, a quill, and a thin strip of ancient-looking paper.

Athena repeated the promises I'd ask her to make and stated that by blood, she was bound to them, with Artemis and Apollo serving as her witnesses. She cut her finger, squeezed several drops into the bowl, and then dipped the quill in, using the liquid as ink to write down her vows. Then she turned around and slid it toward me, picking up the knife and handing it over.

I took it. The handle was warm. "Your blood goes in the other side of the bowl. You write your agreement below mine, that you will faithfully attempt to resurrect my child."

"You really think I can?" She was betting an awful lot on an unproven ability.

"I would not be here, and you'd be dead already, if I thought otherwise."

It was now or never. I glanced at my father again, then over my shoulder at the door. Horus wasn't coming. Sebastian . . . he would be here soon, I hoped. I faced the altar, slit my finger, and then wrote my promise. Athena took the paper and snapped her fingers, and flames began to eat away at the edges, releasing a blood-tinged smoke that rose up in the shape of our words and then disappeared.

In the ensuing silence, the distant sounds of the battle ebbed into the church. Doubt skated along my nerves. Doubt that I could do something so unusual. I'd changed Sebastian back, but he'd been stone for a short period of time, and I'd been hyped up on adrenaline and emotion. This child had been trapped in stone for a thousand years. . . .

My father cleared his throat, the sound bouncing around the lofty space. I knew that was to remind me of my training, of everything I'd learned so far. *Okay. Focus, Ari. You do this right and Athena is gone for good. Out of your life. Out of your father's life. Out of New 2 for good.*

"Okay," I breathed. I could do this. I reached out and placed my hand palm down over the baby's chest. My eyelids slid closed, and with that I imagined a wall, one that held my power, falling down. My curse rose fast, always there, just lurking, waiting for the opportunity to strike, my power growing more volatile and impatient with every day.

All right, Selkirk, do your thing.

Twenty-Three

The doors behind me banged open so hard, one split and the other flew off its hinges. I spun around. A wizened old figure appeared in the doorway, shuffling in with his staff to support him, a hood drawn over his head.

The River Witch stopped in the aisle.

What the hell?

Athena came around the altar and stopped next to me, livid. The witch lifted his wrinkled hand and pulled back his hood. My heart stopped. As the hood was dragged slowly off his head, the old face changed, like he'd peeled away a layer of deceit, leaving behind a beautiful woman with red hair, porcelain skin, and the features of an angel. *A pretty witch*, Crank's voice reminded me. Had she somehow seen beyond the disguise?

And if the kids *had* left with her, then where the hell were they?

The cloak dropped to the floor. The witch was dressed for battle, her hair braided at the sides and pulled away from her face, her staff at the ready. A strange shimmering black breast-plate was molded to her body, covering her torso, neck, and arms. Ancient designs filled the plate.

"Hello, Athena," she said with such underlying pleasure I knew we were all going to be in a world of hurt.

Athena marched off the altar and down the aisle like vengeance reborn. As she reached out to grab the witch, the witch held up her hand, and Athena stopped. Just *froze*.

"How *dare* you interrupt!" Athena railed. "You, more than anyone, know what I have lost!"

"Aye, and I lost too. Or do you forget? You stole *my* child! Mine! Did you think Zeus wouldn't notice you switched our children? You sacrificed *my* child to save your own, and it didn't even work! He knew and took yours anyway. Do you know what he did to my child? He tossed her from the window of his temple, just threw her away."

"You betrayed me first! You should have kept your mouth shut and kept the prophecy to yourself. You knew what would happen once you uttered those words, Dora! You damn well knew it would be the end of my child!"

The River Witch was Anesidora. The Pandora of legend.

Athena's first creation, and the one who'd uttered the fateful prophecy about Athena's child.

Kieran moved to my side as Artemis and Apollo held arrows notched against the strings of their bows, but had yet to raise them. Menai, I noticed, had appeared at the broken doors, her bow drawn as well.

"These long years I have waited, satisfied in the knowledge that I took your child from you, that your attempt to save your child failed. But then when she came along"—Dora flicked a glance at me—"I knew I'd have the most glorious justice. Do you know the rest of the prophecy, gorgon?" she asked me. "That *child* will be sought and found by those wanting to ignite the Blood Wars. He will lead an army against the gods. He is of goddess and vampire, able to consume the blood of the gods, to draw their very essence into his body. And Zeus was the first fated to fall. Do you really want that evil walking this earth?" She turned to Athena. "I *had* to tell. Your son put all of us in danger."

"My son is not evil!" Fury shook Athena's voice. Ironic coming from a goddess who had embraced evil ever since her child was taken. But it also meant the baby's father was not Horus. So why the hell was he here and wanting to kill Athena?

The father was a vampire. Athena had not denied it. So who was he? Then I remembered what Sebastian had learned from his mother's things. Josephine's grandfather had been captured by

Athena. In the tenth century. The attempted murder of her child by Zeus and subsequent War of the Pantheons also occurred in the tenth century. Could Josephine's grandfather have fathered the child? Could that be the source of Josephine's hatred for Athena?

"Now it matters not," Dora said. "Your son will live, but he won't live beyond this night."

Athena broke through Dora's power and slammed her palm against Dora's solar plexus, sending the witch flying backward. She slammed into the massive organ on the second-story balcony. Athena spun around, her eyes blazing at me. "You. Protect my son."

Stunned by what was happening, I didn't answer. Athena appeared right in front of me, her hand squeezing my throat. "I do not make bargains unless I have insurance. Melinoe is in the Underworld right now with your mother's soul. You protect my child and we complete our bargain, or her soul is obliterated."

Athena's bright, angry gaze fell on Kieran. "And you, Celt. Think you, your brothers and sisters are safe in the afterlife? Get in my way and they're all destroyed." Done with her threats, Athena turned back to the organ. She had a witch to kill.

As she swept past Artemis she said, "Watch Ari, don't let her leave." To Apollo, she said, "You're with me."

They strode down the aisle, then leaped onto the second-story balcony and wrenched Dora from the broken organ. As the pipes knocked and fell, earsplitting tones reverberated through the church.

"What the hell happened to Horus?" Kieran asked.

Artemis's head whipped around, her eyes wide. "Horus is here?"

I didn't answer.

"No," she breathed, her face going pale. Artemis ran toward Menai, grabbing her daughter and pulling her to the corner, their heads bowed together.

Athena threw Dora to the aisle below. The witch smashed into the tile, leaving a small crater. Dora's chest and stomach shook. She was laughing. Slowly she pushed to her feet, ducking supernaturally fast as Apollo's arrow blew past her head. "Come to me, my horrors, my spites and vices. Come out and defend me."

The strange, high-pitched sounds I'd heard outside Josephine's house came zipping through the door and into the church, trailing lights and peals of laughter. I remembered why they'd sounded familiar. I'd heard them another time too. At the River Witch's house in the bayou, in the clay jars.

"What are those?" Kieran asked.

"I think those are the things that escaped Dora's jar."

"Some," Dora said, somehow overhearing me. "Not all . . ."

The vices and spites transformed from tiny lights into hideous monsters, demons straight from hell with huge, muscular black bodies, light spilling from cracks in their skin. Athena cursed, attacking the horrors with Apollo. When one was shot through the forehead with an arrow, it simply pulled it out the other side and kept fighting. When Athena shot another with lightning, it burst into a million tiny sparks only to re-form.

There were six in all. Athena finally managed to obliterate one of Dora's creatures. It burst into bits of fiery light, then condensed into one tiny spark to re-form, but she caught it in her hand and smashed it against the wall. The horrors left us alone; they did not approach the altar at all. Hurrying, I ran around the table and reached up to touch my father's bloody boots. I wrapped my hands around the arrow's shaft. "Do it," he insisted. "Hurry."

I couldn't pull the arrow back through his feet, so I snapped the shaft, then grabbed his feet and shoved them upward to his hiss of pain. It was over quickly. His feet free, I climbed up the statue of St. Paul, which flanked the column my father was bound to. I reached for the tie around his wrist. Kieran followed my lead and was climbing the statue of St. Peter on the other side to get to the other wrist.

Just as I reached the knot, Kieran's warning came. "Ari . . ."

I was yanked backward, landing with a thud on the carpet below. *Goddamn it!* Dora dragged me up. Athena screamed her frustration. Menai notched an arrow and sent it at Dora, but the witch swatted it away, the horrors blocking the gods from reaching her.

"You will resurrect that child," she said with a sneer. "I want Athena to suffer, to hold her child in her arms and watch him die, like I did at the bottom of that damn mountain. I want her to feel the loss of a thousand years, and then know what it's like to see him die in front of her eyes. It's called revenge, gorgon. An eye for an eye. Do you not want the same for those you have loved and lost?"

I opened my mouth, but no answer came out.

A lion's roar shook the cathedral. In the doorway, Horus appeared with his black lioness. His eerie eyes were furious, and they zeroed in on Dora. It didn't take much to figure out that the reason he'd been delayed was because of her. "Think you to hold a *god*?" he shouted at Dora. As he marched down the aisle, his linen clothes transformed into Egyptian war garb. The sight made my mouth drop open.

Dora shoved me away and hurried to face him. Artemis moved back into the shadows, but Horus saw her and threw out a hand. She hit the wall and was pinned there, unable to move. He never took his eyes off Dora. "Think you *that* powerful, witch?"

"I waylaid you, didn't I?" Dora answered, her confidence unbelievable.

Athena smashed the last of Dora's horrors and jumped from

the balcony, landing behind Horus, putting him between Dora and herself. The shit was about to hit the fan, and I needed to get my father off that high altar.

"What do you think, brother?" Athena said to Apollo as I inched around the table and back toward my father. "Shall we take them together, or shall I make my peace with Dora once and for all while you visit with the Egyptian?"

Apollo and Horus stared at each other, neither seeming impressed by the other. "Horus and I have a few scores to settle. Have at it, sister," Apollo said, never taking his eyes off his target.

Horus's eyebrow lifted. "It's your funeral."

And then the shit hit the fan. Pews and prayer books went flying. I scrambled up the statue and sliced through the ties with Athena's blade. As Kieran climbed the other statue and used her sword to cut my father's other binding, I went to his feet and held him as best I could. He dropped like a stone, landing half on top of me. We ducked behind the altar table.

"As soon as we have a clear path, we run for the side door," I said.

Athena shot a bolt of lightning at Dora. It ricocheted off her breastplate and slammed into one of the columns supporting the balcony above. The entire left gallery groaned and sagged.

Horus sent Apollo flying into the pews, his body blasting through them like a plow eating up dirt. Pews were shoved so far forward that they blocked the side door. "Do you know another way out of here?" I asked Kieran.

"Around the corner, I think. There might be a door that leads behind the altar and into the garden."

Horus focused his attention on Athena, grabbing her from behind and flinging her backward. She crashed through one of the columns on the second floor. Wasting no time, Horus jumped up after her.

"Okay, now's our chance," I said. "Ready?"

We went to go, but Horus and Athena fell to the floor, barring our path. He got up first.

"Horus, no," Artemis begged from her imprisonment on the wall. That he was able to keep her there and hold his own in a fight spoke to his power. Frustration radiated from him. He growled, hauled back, and punched Athena so hard she tumbled back over the pews, heels over head. Artemis screamed and cursed at him.

An arrow struck him in the shoulder. Horus swung around. Menai stood near the exit. He seemed incredulous that she'd shot him, like her doing so meant something significant, a kind of betrayal of sorts. "Leave her alone!" Artemis shouted, fear in her voice.

"Like I would hurt my child," Horus growled at her as he yanked the arrow from his shoulder. *Holy shit.* Horus was

Menai's father. Now it made sense. The child he was coming for wasn't the baby, but Menai. And apparently, he held Athena and Artemis accountable for some wrongdoing. Horus reached down and grabbed Athena by the throat as she struggled to her feet. Blood poured from her nose.

Horus's lion leaped over the broken pews and lunged at Menai. Menai shot another arrow. In midair, the lioness transformed into a cat, the arrow missing, and then it was back to the lioness, slamming into Menai. Artemis screamed, struggling against Horus's hold even as the god fought against Athena, while Dora and more of her horrors dealt with Apollo.

Horus commanded the lioness, and instead of ripping out Menai's throat, the large beast lay on Menai's chest, pinning her to the floor. Menai's curses and struggles didn't seem to bother the lioness.

"Go, go, go," I whispered, and we crouched down, hurrying away from the altar.

Dora disappeared, then reappeared in front of us. Athena shot another bolt, and it hit the statue of Jesus perched on the peak of the high altar. It cracked, chunks smashing into the ground next to the altar, and way too close to the Hands. Dora dragged me to the altar, sending Kieran airborne with a wave of her hand.

But Kieran stopped, hovering in the air for a second before slowly being set down. Sebastian, his face and clothes covered in blood, stood in the doorway. He looked like some ancient god of death, his gray eyes burning like molten silver. I knew Zaria must've died a gruesome death.

On her feet, Kieran ran to my father, as Sebastian strode down the aisle, ignoring the fighting around him, his gaze locked on mine. But a horror jumped in his path as Dora shoved me at the table.

Athena screamed her fury. She ran for Dora, tackling her to the ground and knocking the table hard as Apollo slammed into it after a punch from Horus. The Hands were hit and went flying high into the air.

Athena was pinned beneath Dora, but her sharp gaze found me immediately. "Do it! Do it now!"

"Yes! Do it!" Dora sneered, throwing Athena off, grabbing my father with an invisible hand. In a blink he was flat on his back on the altar table with a dagger raised at his heart. "Do it!"

The Hands crested in the air and began to fall. In those two seconds, a hundred thoughts went through my mind. I had to be touching the statue. I couldn't do it from this distance. My father was going to die.

And then Mel's incorporeal form solidified, holding a soul over her palm. My heart gave a grief-stricken thud at the sight of my mother's soul. My father saw it, his face breaking in despair, the struggle going out of him.

"Eleni," I heard him say, the barest of whispers.

My gaze flew back to the Hands. No time. I staggered up and ran, the pounding of my heart the only thing I could hear as my power tore through me, ripping me open. My eyes burned. In my peripheral vision, I saw some shield their eyes. But that was just a blink in time as the gorgon surged up and out of me with a force that snapped my head back and made my body arch.

I screamed through the burn of energy searing through my veins, lashing cruel and complete, finally set free. Through a cloudy haze, I slid beneath the basket, colliding with Athena as she did the same.

The basket landed in my arms.

Sebastian was suddenly beside me, his hand on my arm, concern in his eyes. Mine were dry and hot. I blinked them hard, trying to erase the blurriness. And then I felt the basket change from stone to reeds.

TWENTY-FOUR

THE HANDS HOLDING THE BASKET—ZEUS'S HANDS—began to change as well. I shook the basket and they fell off, landing with a sickening slap on the tile.

Quiet filled the church. The only sounds were heaving breaths, the occasional falling of plaster and debris, and the chaos from outside.

Until Dora's laughter flowed through the nave, carrying the sick tone of cruelty and delight. Athena crawled over, her eyes big with hope. She tugged the basket to her and looked inside. The child was still stone. Misery twisted her features. "No! It didn't work!" She lifted her head, her green eyes darkening as she found me. She was laid bare, all of it there, the torment, the grief, the raw defeat. And then the rage came. "You *idiot*! It didn't work!"

She came at me, hitting me hard and sending us tumbling down the two sanctuary steps and into the aisle. She straddled me, hands around my neck and squeezing. Sebastian lunged, but Apollo tackled him in a bear hug. I grabbed Athena's wrists, lungs straining, pressure building in my face, and through all the pain and fear, I couldn't miss her devastation, her thousand-year-old sorrow coming through her madness. My heart was hammering, and it burned with . . . sympathy . . . because I knew the outcome. I knew as my power uncoiled and snaked through my body, aware, this time not leaping up for a quick strike, but building, slithering down my arms and into my hands and fingertips.

Our eyes met. Her squeezing stilled. She knew too. And it didn't feel good, to know I was going to kill her, to see the realization, the desolation and acceptance, the weariness in her eyes.

The blast that flowed out of me was hot and all-consuming. She let go and pushed off, stumbling to her feet and walking a few steps away as I sat up. Everyone had gone still. Stopping in the aisle, Athena glanced over at Artemis, who'd been released by Horus and was openly crying, and then at her brother, his arms still around Sebastian, his eyes glassy too.

She loved them. They loved her.

As messed up as Athena had become, they'd stood by her.

Then she turned slightly and looked toward the basket sitting on the sanctuary steps as her body began to harden.

A tiny cry echoed in the church.

A baby's cry.

Frantic horror filled Athena's eyes and my heart. *Oh God. If she'd just waited, just let my power work through a thousand years of stone!* And now she was dying as her baby lived. Spurred by an intention I didn't fully understand, I crawled on my hands and knees to the basket. A beautiful baby boy gazed up at me with round green eyes, his chubby arms moving up and down.

Carefully I lifted him from the basket and took him to his mother. Marble had eaten its way up her shoulders. The love in her eyes made my throat ache as she stared at her child. Her living child, with pudgy cheeks, perfect lips, bright-green eyes, and a fuzz of soft black hair on his head. "Turn me back," she begged in a broken, choked voice, tears filling her eyes and spilling over. "Please, turn me back."

I found myself reaching out to touch her, to save her. Yet my power didn't leap to life. It was muted, depleted. It needed a little time. And time was against us. But still I tried.

I expected hate or anger when she realized it was over, but Athena simply returned her attention to her son, the child she loved above all else. He gazed up at her and made a cute baby sound, and then he smiled.

"Archer, my son . . . ," she whispered, marble closing over her lips, her cheeks, freezing the tears on her face, then claiming the color of her eyes.

And she was gone. Athena was gone.

For a moment no one moved or spoke. Then Dora snorted. "Not exactly how I pictured it happening, but satisfying nonetheless. Nice touch, letting her see what she'd be missing. I believe I've grown a new respect for you, gorgon."

I hiked the baby higher on my hip. "I didn't do it to hurt her; I did it to . . ." How could I explain? I hated Athena, what she'd done to my family and so many others, but in her moment of pure suffering and heartbreak, I could not bask in her pain. I'm not sure what that made me, but I couldn't help but think of my mother. What she would have given to see me one last time. The baby cooed and gurgled, its chubby arms and legs jerking, delighting in moving. And I knew I'd done the right thing.

Dora still had the knife poised over my father's chest. "You'd better step away from my father, witch," I said, deadly calm, before turning to Mel. "Take my mother back." Mel nodded in a daze, shocked Athena was gone. As she disappeared, I held on to the image of my mother's beautiful, bright soul, committing it to memory.

Apollo released Sebastian and shot out his hand. His bow, which had dropped amid the damaged pews, flew into his hand.

Artemis and Menai raised their bows, arrows pointed at Dora. Horus joined them, a blade appearing in his hand and lengthening into a wicked curve. His action garnered him a surprised look from Apollo and Menai, but not from Artemis. She just dipped her head in thanks.

"I'm starting to believe no one likes me," Dora said flatly.

"No one ever did," Artemis shot back.

"Except my maker. And you all just hated that, didn't you? That I was Athena's favorite? I loved her above all others! *Me!* And what does she do but betray my trust, betray me by offering my child in place of hers."

"You're mad," Apollo said coldly. "You could not have stood against Athena, nor can you stand against us."

Dora rolled her eyes. "Think I would come here, set all this in motion if I wasn't protected, if I didn't think I could win? You seem to forget the Aegis your dear sister dropped into the waves when she set her hurricanes upon this city."

"You have Zeus's Aegis, his shield," Artemis said, disbelieving. Horus cursed.

"What?" Dora glanced down at her armor. "Did you think this was just a pretty piece to wear into a battle? It is more than that. I found it. I made it better. I gave it *life*. I am a witch of great power, trained by Hecate and Athena alike. I took Zeus's Aegis and stripped its Titan god skin; it is the skin that gives the shield its power, and I nurtured it, grew a tiny egg into something new in the womb of the Titan skin and the bayou. A living shield." She laughed. "My very own shield maiden. A living, breathing Titan."

The hell?

"Violet. Show yourself, my dear."

The breath whooshed out of me.

I watched, horrified, as the strange breastplate withdrew from Dora like a shroud, pooling in front of the altar, growing higher and more substantial until it became Violet. Our Violet.

Dear God. Violet was a Titan?

"Now," Dora said, "I want that child. I want it dead like mine."

My gaze went to Violet. She'd been raised in the bayou by Dora. I couldn't wrap my head around it, but I knew one thing: I would never let Dora lay a hand on the child in my arms. "Bring me the child," Dora demanded, her wicked eyes locked with mine.

It was on the tip of my tongue to tell her to suck it. My anger was rising. I swallowed, holding the baby a little tighter, my hand going to the back of its soft head as it looked over my shoulder at whatever was behind me. "You've had your revenge, Dora," I said, my attention flicking between her and Violet, who waited so quietly beside the altar. "It's over. Athena's separated from her child forever, just as you are from yours."

Dora's expression went shrewd. "Unless you change her back.

And we can't have that now, can we?" Her hand shot out, power surging straight for me. I covered the baby and spun as Dora's power hit the statue of Athena square in the chest. It toppled to the sounds of her siblings' shouts. It happened so fast. Athena crashed to the floor and shattered even as Apollo slid down to catch her. He was too late.

In disbelief, I swung around to Dora. The patient man that my father was, he'd waited for the perfect opportunity to strike. Dora was without her shield. In a flash, he grabbed Dora's hand that held her knife, spun off the table, and was around her back, holding the knife to her throat before I could blink.

But Dora was just a fraction quicker, tracing to the front of the altar as my father went to slide the blade across her throat.

"Violet, to me," Dora commanded.

With a solemn look my way, Violet dispersed and her darkness latched onto Dora, clutching her, this time covering her from ankle to neck and coming over her head to protect her skull and face, leaving only her eyes, nostrils, and mouth visible.

Damn it.

We couldn't hurt Dora without hurting Violet.

High-pitched laugher filtered through the cathedral again, zipping and zinging and gathering behind Dora. More spites and vices. *Great.* My father shoved Kieran behind him.

"Get me that child and the gorgon," Dora barked.

The horrors flew at me, and it was then that the full force of my predicament hit me. I had a *baby* in my arms. A tiny being to protect. Cradling him against my chest, I bolted down the aisle, leaping over debris, heading for the door, panic spurring me on. *Almost there.*

The next thing I knew Henri and Dub were there, running through the vestibule toward me, both angry and itching for a fight. "That stupid witch locked us—"

"Fight the horrors!" I yelled. "Violet is on Dora, don't hurt her!"

They gave me incredulous, confused looks, but there wasn't time to explain. A horror landed in front of the exit, blocking my path. I veered right. And I learned very quickly that one way to destroy Dora's horrors was by fire. Dub came in very handy. He and Henri ran to my father and Kieran, my father using her sword against one of the spites.

Dora appeared in front of me. I slid to a stop.

"Violet," I said, backing away, trying to get through to her as Athena's baby sensed my panic and started to cry. "Don't let her do this." But Dora had raised Violet. Dora was the only mother she'd ever known. But still, I tried. "Don't let her take this baby. Please, Violet."

I was powerless, unable to risk turning Violet to stone along with Dora.

"Goddamn it, Vi!" Dub yelled. "Get the hell off that witch!"

Henri shouted Violet's name too. So did Sebastian.

Dora snatched my arm in her cold grip. I knew the horrors were keeping the others busy. I was on my own. No sooner did I have that thought than Sebastian wrapped an arm around my waist. He pulled against Dora's hold. She pulled back.

"Don't," he said to her in that powerful voice, the kind that could stop armies. She hesitated, his power working to slow her, but with Violet's protection, it had very little effect otherwise.

From the corner of my eye, I saw the lioness slinking down the far side of the nave, her steady gaze on Dora. Hunting. Dora laughed at Sebastian's attempt to reach for the baby. I pulled free. Sebastian shoved us behind him. There was a reason the Aegis had made Zeus and Athena invincible. It seemed to not only protect, but to diminish another's power.

Dora sent Sebastian flying. He slammed into one of the columns, shearing it in half. One side of the balcony groaned and dropped a few feet, threatening to collapse.

"Ari, duck!" I shielded the baby and ducked at Menai's warning.

Two of her arrows zipped mere inches from my head. Dora spun just in time, and they glanced off the back of her head. She hauled me up.

Damn if I was handing over the child. With every cry it made, my protective instincts increased. I wasn't letting him go.

Her hand snaked around my throat, the other grabbing on to the child.

"Violet," I pleaded.

"She can't betray me."

The lioness leaped onto Dora's back, her massive paws clutching Dora's shoulder and her giant mouth latching onto her skull. The force sent us sprawling. My hold over the baby loosened as I stumbled over a pew, grappling to maintain my grip on the child.

Damn it. No!

As I fell, I flailed for the baby. Falcon wings swooped blazing fast over us, claws latched on to the baby as I hit the ground, the breath knocked out of me and pain shooting through my side, the place where Athena had stabbed me only two weeks earlier. I glanced down. A large wooden splinter had pierced my side.

The lioness's brutal snarls grabbed my attention as Horus transformed from falcon to god, the baby in his arms. Relieved, I focused on Dora. She was on her back but reached for her staff and shoved it against the lioness, sending the beast sailing across the room.

Quickly I searched the ground, knowing I had to move now, before she got up. *There.* One of the arrows Menai had shot. I swiped it and bolted, tackling Dora to the floor just as she started to rise. Before she could react, I shoved the arrow into her eye and drove it deep into her brain.

Her body shook, her legs flailing. But I held the arrow still, her words whispering out of a bloody mouth with a chuckle, "I die . . . and she dies with me."

Horror slashed through me.

Denial built in my throat. *Oh God.* Hot tears rose, blurring my vision as I shook Dora's armor-clad shoulders. "Violet!" Sebastian knelt beside me. "Somebody help her!" I cried.

The cathedral had gone silent as Artemis and Apollo dispatched the last of the horrors.

Everyone stared at us like it was a done deal. Dora was dying and Violet with her.

Horus handed the baby to Artemis and slid down beside me, bloodied and breathing hard, to take stock of the situation. A small tool appeared in his hand, and he shoved it up Dora's nose. My stomach rolled. I grabbed his forearm. "Stop. What are you doing?"

"Making sure she stays dead."

"No!"

Before I could stop him, he pulled chunks of brain matter out of her nostril and tossed them in the aisle as bile rose to my throat and my gut rolled. To Dub he commanded, "Burn it."

Pale and obviously shaken, Dub set fire to Anesidora's brains. "Try coming back from that," he muttered.

The baby was safe in Artemis's arms. Everyone was okay.

Except Violet. I'd killed Violet. Dear God, I killed Violet. I bent over Dora's body, my forehead falling on her shoulder, and cried. "Please come back. Violet, just come back."

"Come on, Vi, you're a Titan," Sebastian joined in. "You're stronger than Dora. Come back to us."

"And what about Pascal?" Dub dropped down beside me, placing his hand on the armor covering Dora's skull. "Who's going to take care of him?"

"We'll need help picking out a new house. A bigger, grander mansion with gold fittings and safes filled with jewels," Henri added, standing over us, his eyes bright with tears. Menai put her hand on his shoulder.

Nothing happened. No matter what we said, nothing happened.

My heart shrank to a hard, painful knot. God, it hurt. My fists clenched, a scream building, pushing against my chest. I sobbed, unable to hold it in. Goddamn it, Violet was gone. *Gone!*

Dub was crying. Tears filled Sebastian's eyes, and I heard Henri sniffling behind me. My father's hands fell on my shoulders. He spoke to me, but I didn't hear him—inside was so loud and chaotic, filled with crushing guilt and raging grief.

"You're gods," I accused. "Why can't you do something?"

Horus pointed at me. "Do *not* turn those eyes on us, gorgon," he warned.

I flinched, my hands going to my face. My eyes burned. They were hot and angry from crying, and maybe from something else. "Then help her," I begged.

Artemis hiked the baby on her hip. "We cannot remove her. She's a Titan. A shield. A living one, with a mind of her own, and a will of her own. We have no power over her."

The black shield covering Dora was warm to the touch. I kept my hands on Dora's shoulders, wishing with everything I had that Violet would hear us. We stayed, gathered around her, not knowing what else to do.

I had no idea how much time had passed when my father's voice finally reached me. "Come, Ari." Spent and numb, I let him help me to my feet. My friends rose with me, looking as lost and sad as I felt.

"We have matters to discuss," Horus started. "My bargain with you," he told Sebastian. "The child. Your city." Then he looked at Artemis, challenging her to oppose him. "Us."

She kept quiet, but her look said she definitely had something to say about that. Artemis ignored Horus and smiled gently at me. "You wish your curse removed."

I nodded woodenly, unable to speak, unable to care.

Tears shone through Artemis's smile. "She was my sister. I know what she knew. I know the words spoken and I can untangle them."

"Why would you?" Henri asked. "You've been in league with Athena all this time."

The question was hard for the gods to answer. "We loved her," Apollo finally said with a shrug.

"She was good once, kind," Artemis tried to explain. "My sister had moments of her old self. But she was wounded inside. Broken. We stood by her because we loved her. Because she needed us. Her son is named in our honor. We are both"—she held up her bow and gestured to Apollo's—"archers. We couldn't bring ourselves to be among the many who'd turned their backs and betrayed her."

In some ways, I guess I understood their decision. In others, not so much. But they were gods. Their viewpoints, decisions, and ideas on humanity, family, love, were bound to not be fully understandable by the rest of us mere mortals. I let out a heavy sigh, my gaze falling on the baby, sorry for his losses. His parents were gone, his grandfather tried to murder him, and the future held portents of blood and war. Poor thing was starting out life with a lot of baggage.

"I want that big Victorian," a small voice said behind me, "the one with all the towers, the one on the corner of Coliseum and Fourth."

A zing of hope rocketed through my veins. *God, please don't let me be imagining . . .* I turned slowly, holding my breath, heart leaping, to see Violet standing next to Dora's body. The lioness came over and stood next to Violet, their shoulders even in height. It sniffed her cheek, its nostrils puffing in and out. Violet smiled, dipping her head like it tickled.

My legs went weak. She was okay. We went to her en masse, Henri saying, "It's yours, *chère*. We'll fill it with gowns and masks and all things shiny."

Dub hugged Violet. "And we'll get a new pool for Pascal." Sebastian and I exchanged teary smiles over Dub's head.

Violet stared at us all, a small smile on her face, before her look became thoughtful. "What's a Titan?"

Before we could react, quick footsteps near the main doors had us all shooting to our feet. Michel, Bran, and Rowen entered with a small contingent of bloodied fighters behind them. They took stock of the situation, confusion and surprise lighting their war-weary eyes at the sight of the church and the gathering of gods. Kieran hurried around us to Bran. Relief filled his weary eyes, and he enveloped her in a huge hug, lifting her off her feet.

"I must call off Athena's army," Apollo said, marching down the debris-littered aisle.

"Ari," Artemis prompted. "Are you ready?"

I turned to her. "Yes. I'm ready."

"And you, Mistborn?" Horus asked. Sebastian nodded and walked away from the group with the Egyptian god.

Artemis handed the baby to Menai, and then faced me. "Thank you. For the kindness you showed my sister."

Untangling my curse was a quiet affair, full of words and power that hung and built and danced in the air, swirling through the church and around me, finally through me—pulling and tugging at my core, my veins, my cells, at everything I was. It was uncomfortable. Not painful, though it might have been. Yet the untangling was significant enough to send me to my knees. I didn't know if Artemis was making it less painful or not, but if she did, I was grateful.

The curse came out of me slowly and grudgingly, words separating themselves from my being, swirling, old and ancient, and finally untangling themselves and dispersing, leaving me empty for a blink before a great energy rushed in, filling every corner of me with heat. My chest expanded; it felt like my heart would explode. Electricity zipped beneath my skin, traveling to the tips of my fingers and toes.

I bent forward, my hands hitting the floor. *Dear God. What is she doing to me?* The sensations finally faded, leaving me weak, sweaty, and panting.

When I was finally able to lift my head, I was met with Artemis's gentle smile. "A kindness repaid with a kindness."

I frowned in confusion. "What did you do to me?"

"Removed your gorgon curse, but left you with its power."

Stunned, I sat back on my heels, shaking. "Why would you do that?" Why would she leave a god-killer in existence?

"Because even the gods need checks and balances. And we might have need of you when the Blood Wars come."

I blew out a heavy breath, the reality setting in. Truly, unbelievably setting in. I was free. It was over. And I still had power to protect myself and those I loved. I glanced at Sebastian and he joined me with a deep, happy smile, one that made me laugh as he reached down and helped me up, enveloping me in his arms. I held on tight, still reeling. "It's gone," I said against his neck. "The monster is gone."

Over his shoulder, my father smiled broadly, some of the deep sadness that always lurked in his eyes gone. I hugged him, too. He squeezed me hard. "Your mother would be so proud of you. I am proud of you."

"Great. The girl's going to be more insufferable than ever," Menai commented, amusement in her eyes. I shot her the middle finger. She laughed and shot one right back.

Apollo returned as Bran, Michel, and my father began discussing the state of things beyond the cathedral walls. Artemis handed Apollo the child. He looked panicked for a moment, but then his face transformed, going soft, a smile tugging his lips apart as he walked off, cooing. Seeing a big, powerful Greek god taken with a tiny baby made me smile.

Horus and Artemis moved to the back wall to talk in private.

"So what's that all about?" I asked Menai.

She observed her mother and Horus. It struck me then that Menai was a full-blown goddess. She had two heavyweights for parents. "He's livid with her for staying with Athena. For rejecting him and choosing her over him."

"Why did she?" Henri asked.

Menai shrugged. "When my mother became pregnant with me, she knew Athena would go mad with the hurt of seeing me around every day. Even though I was born seven hundred years after her child, my mother was afraid for me. She wanted to withdraw from the temple, to go with my father, but Athena begged her to stay, to let them raise me together, to help heal the loss of her own child through me. I think it got pretty intense, like dangerous, for my mother and me. So she promised Athena she'd stay. Athena wanted proof of her promise, so my mother confided in Athena the secret name my father gave me when I was born—it's an Egyptian thing. But it holds a lot of power over that person."

"So the hold over Artemis was you."

Menai nodded. "It didn't help that Athena hated my father— he was one of a few gods she hadn't been able to overthrow during the War of the Pantheons. And my father was so pissed he couldn't stand it. Apparently, he wanted to punish my mother for even considering staying with Athena, so he removed himself not only from our life, but from the world. A rash decision I'm sure he regrets. He'll want her now. There's nothing in their way anymore."

"Will she go?"

"I don't know. She loves him. She's loved him all this time."

Menai watched her parents, lost in her thoughts. Sebastian had gone over to talk with his father. Michel glanced at the baby Bran was now holding, disbelief passing through his eyes. Now he knew. The child was half Arnaud. Part of Sebastian's family. Fated to start the Blood Wars.

Artemis shouted, "Fine!" drawing my attention.

Horus's hands were on his hips, and he appeared as angry and frustrated as Artemis was. "Fine!" he shot back.

They marched back to Menai. "We're going to be a family," she said, angry. "Half the year on Olympus, half in Egypt."

"What about me?" Menai asked, and from her tone, I realized that she thought they were leaving her.

Horus frowned. "What about you? You're coming with us whether you like it or not. We have a couple hundred years to make up for." He rubbed his shoulder where she'd shot him. "And we'll need to talk about some ground rules."

Menai swallowed, but I saw the flash of surprise in her eyes. But she was her mother's daughter, and her eyebrow cocked in challenge. "I want him to come visit me without *you* giving him a hard time," she said, gesturing to a very astonished Henri.

Artemis suppressed a grin as Horus's face paled and went a little confounded—he was in territory he probably hadn't been in for a very long time. His gaze narrowed on Henri. "We'll take a flight sometime, you and I, to lay some ground rules of our own, eh?"

Henri swallowed. "Yes, sir."

"That leaves us with the child," Apollo said. "As much as I like the little thing, I'm not babysitting for six months while you're in Egypt."

"You won't have to," Artemis said. "We'll take Archer with us."

"Or you can leave him here while you're gone," Sebastian suggested. "He's my family too, unless I'm wrong."

"No," Artemis admitted. "You're not wrong." She exchanged a glance with Apollo. Obviously the thought that Archer's other family might want to be a part of his life had never had occurred to them. But Sebastian had a claim.

"He should be raised by both families," Sebastian said. "You and Apollo for six months in Olympus, and us for six months here."

"Is that good for a kid, though?" I asked. "To go from one family to another like that?"

"If that's how he's raised," Michel said. "If that's all he ever knows. If both families give him a good home, work together—visiting, communicating—we can, quite possibly, change his fate. Change the outcome of the Blood Wars. Or stop them from even starting."

"The Blood Wars are coming regardless," Apollo said. "I have seen it. But . . . I think you're right. We raise him, give him a true and loyal family. And when the wars come, that loyalty will be returned. Archer will fight with us, alongside the gods."

"When are the wars coming?" Dub asked, fear in his tone.

"There's time enough for us to raise the child. But in that time, we must begin the search for those gods Athena imprisoned and free them. Our numbers have dwindled, thanks to the war she waged. We'll need every god we can find to fight the threat I've seen coming."

The gods began talking about all the changes that would have to be made in their pantheon. They spoke of opening the way for us to travel freely into their realm in order to be part of Archer's life. When all was said and done, they'd worked out a schedule. Archer would go to Olympus with Apollo, Artemis, Horus, and Menai for six months. Sebastian, Michel, and the rest of us would be able to visit as we pleased, to form a relationship so that when the baby was in our world the following six months, he would be content with his caretakers.

Sebastian was sincere in his desire to be part of the baby's life, and it made me see him in a new way. He'd only had his father and Josephine, but now the baby provided a direct Arnaud link to his mother's side of the family. It was a link I was certain he wanted to strengthen. Sebastian wanted roots just like I did. I glanced at my father and the kids. It seemed like we were both getting our wish.

After the gods departed with little Archer, we left the cathedral.

I steeled myself for what I knew would greet me. But still the sight brought a deep well of sadness. The once beautiful square was littered with the dead and dying. Buildings were destroyed, some still burning. We stayed on the steps outside, just taking in the devastation. Violet slipped her hand in mine. I smiled down at her and squeezed, so grateful she was okay. Sebastian's arm brushed against mine.

"What now?" Dub asked.

"First we need to fix our little tourist problem," Bran answered. "Can't have them going past The Rim with tales of gods and monsters."

"Most of them have been gathered at the hospital and other safe locations," Rowen said. "The witches will take care of it. By the time they're done, the tourists won't remember anything but a crazy Mardi Gras party and a bad hangover."

"Thank God for New 2 and Mardi Gras," Henri commented, "where most anything can be explained."

I couldn't argue with that.

"We'll rebuild," Sebastian said. "We'll add schools and health care and shelters for those outside the Quarter. It's time we started caring about more than just the rich Novem families and take care of everyone in New 2."

Michel lifted a brow, pride shining in his gray eyes. "It'll take some work, son, but we can make it happen."

"The Novem, as it was, is too fractured to repair," Bran added. "We'll have to start over, a new council, a new approach. . . ."

Bran, Rowen, and Michel exchanged looks, then fixed their attention on Sebastian. "You in?" Bran asked him.

Sebastian blinked in surprise. He'd fought against his birthright, against being an heir, against being a part of the Novem organization. But now . . . now things were different, and *would* be different. And I could see he knew it too. Everything he had been through . . . it all had given him a unique viewpoint. He wasn't stuck in his entitlement, his wealth, his family connections, and his power as some of the Novem heirs had been. Being a part of a new council with a new way to run the city in which everyone was taken care of . . . I thought he'd be perfect for the task.

I gave him an encouraging grin. He answered them while keeping his gaze on me, his smile going lopsided. "Yeah. I'm in."

TWENTY-FIVE

FOUR DAYS LATER WE MOVED INTO THE MASSIVE VICTORIAN mansion on Coliseum Street, with its tall peaks and lacy iron-and-wood scrollwork. There was a ballroom. A *ballroom*. Violet was already talking about planning the biggest masquerade party New 2 had ever seen.

Granted, the place needed a lot of TLC. The house hadn't been occupied in fifteen years, but I loved the grand foyer, the marble mantels and ornate plaster. Violet had good taste in homes, I'd give her that. There was even a lagoon-style pool in the back that was filled with green algae and years of brackish water and leaves. Pascal was in heaven.

Henri, true to his word, had come home that night with a chest of jewels and presented them to a delighted Violet. When I gave him a look asking where the hell he got them, he shrugged and we left it at that. Every day since the guys came home with masks, gowns, and things they'd found to replace the items Violet had lost in the fire.

I'd lost my mother's letter and the small things she left for me, but in my father, I had more of her than I ever thought possible. Along with Sebastian, my father was becoming very involved in the rebuilding of New 2 and the forming of a new council. He had a new purpose, and a say that others respected, and I was thrilled for him.

Violet and I were busy fixing Crank's room for her arrival. She was itching to get home, so sick of being cooped up in the hospital. After we finished putting clean sheets on the new bed and adding covers and pillows, our job was done. Then it was off to help Violet hang more masks on her wall.

"Do I have a mother and father?" she asked me as I hammered a small nail into the wall. I stopped to face her. She stared at me with those big, dark eyes, a red mask pushed on top of her head. I went to the bed and sat on the edge. "Real ones?" she amended.

Dora had said she grew Violet in the womb of the Aegis and the bayou. "I think you must have. Dora needed something to work with, right? An egg, she said, remember? That egg was you. You had a mother and father. I don't think she created you out of thin air, you know?"

"You really think so?"

I nodded.

She thought about it for a moment. "Then I'm going to find them. Will you help me?"

"Of course I will."

"Maybe there is something at Dora's house, a clue. . . ."

"We'll learn everything we can. Go through it top to bottom. Michel, Rowen, and my father are fixing the Keeper. As soon as the library is back and Presby restored, we'll find out everything we can on the Titans, too. Things the rest of the world doesn't know. I'll read whatever you want me to. And soon you'll learn to read, once school is back in session."

Violet picked up a mask from the pile on the bed and fiddled with the feathers attached to one side. "I thought she was my mother. She never said, but that's what I thought."

It must have been so hard for Violet to hear everything Dora had said. The witch had grown and used Violet for her own protection. But I sensed that Violet loved Dora anyway. It was why she had shielded her and protected her even as we begged her not to.

"I'm sorry," I said. "About what happened."

She tilted her head. "You think I'm still a treasure, a great, shining star?"

I caught her hand and pulled her to the bed so that she was standing in front of me. "More than ever."

A smile finally came. "I will always protect you, Ari. I will look after you."

Tears pricked my eyes. Dora might have created Violet for a terrible purpose, but Violet had a beautiful soul. She was an honest one-of-a-kind. A Titan—though it was still hard to wrap my head around that one. A shield maiden. I hugged her tightly. "Thank you. Same goes."

"Oh jeez, if y'all start breaking into song, I might have to burn something."

Dub lurked in the doorway with Crank, who was on crutches. Henri and Sebastian loomed in the background.

"Crank!"

Violet and I hurried over the gowns and masks to welcome her home.

TWENTY-SIX

HE WAITED UNTIL THE HOUSE WAS QUIET, UNTIL THE KIDS WERE in bed and there'd be no interruptions. He had to talk to her now, to try and resolve things before he went to Olympus tomorrow to see Archer. He knocked, and her muted voice answered from the other side of the bedroom door. Slowly he pushed it open. She turned away from the dresser. The strain and worry that had lurked in her eyes since the day they met was gone. In their place shone a clear turquoise blue.

But as he entered the room, some of the strain came back into her eyes. Because of him, the lies he'd told, the way he'd pushed her away.

Her fingers fiddled with a new top hat in her hand. She placed it on the charred skull of Eugene Hood, one of Dub's decorating contributions from St. Louis Cemetery, and then rearranged the bed of Mardi Gras beads around the skull's base.

"He's grown on you, huh?" he said.

"Yeah. Guess I got used to the creep factor at the other house. My room wouldn't be the same without him staring at me from the dresser." She leaned back, curious and hesitant.

He swallowed. "How do you feel?" She'd gotten what she'd been after. Her curse was gone, and she was free. It still amazed him every time he thought about it.

Her brow furrowed as she thought about her answer. "Normal, I guess. I feel mostly the same, physically. The big change is in here." She tapped her temple. "Still getting used to the idea that it's over. I have a future, you know?" She looked away, then back at him. "Thank you. For helping me. For everything. How do you feel?"

What would she say when he told her? He shoved his hands in his pockets and drew in a deep breath, his nerves having a field day. "The same. I'm still the same, Ari."

It took a moment for the information to sink in. Her face changed, going a tiny bit paler. A frown wrinkled her forehead. "But—" She shook her head.

"I told Horus not to change me back."

"Why?" She breathed the word, holding on to the dresser behind her with both hands.

"Because things changed. When we were fighting in the cathedral . . . And after, with everything that happened . . . Strength, power . . . They have their benefits."

"Benefits," she repeated.

God, this was uncomfortable. "The kind that allow me to protect the people I care about."

She blinked. "You didn't have to do that. You hate—"

"No. I'm making my peace with who I am. And I'm not being some kind of martyr, all right? It wasn't a sacrifice in the way you're thinking. It's for me, too. To know I'm stronger, more powerful than most. I didn't want to give that up. There's security in that. I can stand up to whatever comes our way in the future. It takes some of the worry away, for me, for the kids, the baby . . . you."

Her mouth curved in a rueful smile. "And I ended up with my powers anyway."

"Yeah. Didn't see that one coming. If I had, though, I would've made the same decision."

She licked her bottom lip and bit down, snagging his attention to the faint glisten left behind. His pulse kicked up a notch. Did she really have to do that? Now, when he was trying his damnedest to be good and keep his distance?

Her expression shifted to sad acceptance. Her chin lifted, and she parked a smile on her face. "Okay. So I guess that makes us friends, then."

Wait. "What? No."

"No?"

"No."

Hurt filled her eyes. "I can't, Sebastian. I'm not made that way. To know—"

"I'm not asking you to be okay with me drinking from someone else. I'll get it from a bag. Look, I made mistakes before when I tried to avoid feeding, and I screwed myself big-time. I've already put myself on a regular schedule. I'm making sure I'm supplied, that I won't go crazy like I did before." He ran a hand down his face, wanting desperately for her to understand, to believe in him again. He moved forward, closer, but not too close. "I didn't let you in before, and I'm sorry. I told you I wanted to be in a relationship and then I shut you out. It wasn't fair. I was afraid."

"Afraid?"

"Of turning you off, hurting you, of losing everyone. If you all saw me when I . . . it wasn't pretty. It was ugly and harsh and violent. And it was my fault, because I kept trying to avoid drinking and that made the cravings worse. I . . . I don't know. I was stupid, an ass, whatever you want to call me."

She pushed off the dresser and took a step forward. The scent of her soap and shampoo made his gut tighten. His fingers itched to reach out and touch her, but he forced them still. He had no right to touch her. She'd told him before that she was "done." And he wasn't sure if she still felt that way.

He wanted her to make her own decision, to touch him if she wanted to. He didn't know why, but that was monumentally important to him.

Maybe because by reaching out, she'd be accepting him. And that acceptance would mean more to him than anything.

"I'll make you a deal," she said, looking up at him with an unreadable expression. He swallowed and nodded. "If you are possessed with the urge to drink from anything other than a bag, you come to me."

A spark of hope stirred in his chest. She would help him through any rough times. That was a good sign. A fucking great sign.

"If you need to drink from anyone, it'll be from me, for as long as we're together."

Hope exploded, firing through his chest like a goddamn missile. His heart thumped hard and fast. And when she reached out and placed both of her hands on his hips, he lost it. He totally lost it. He dragged her to him and held on for dear life.